PRAISE FOR THE WOMEN OF THE FAMILY

PRAISE FOR THE WOMEN OF THE FAMILY

by Mahmoud Shukair
translated by Paul Starkey

Interlink Books

An imprint of Interlink Publishing Group, Inc.
Northampton, Massachusetts

First published 2019 by

Interlink Books
An imprint of Interlink Publishing Group, Inc.
46 Crosby Street, Northampton, MA 01060
www.interlinkbooks.com

Library of Congress Cataloging-in-Publication data:
Names: Shuqayr, Maòhmåud, author. | Starkey, Paul, translator.
Title: Praise for the women of the family / by Mahmoud Shukair ; translated
    by Paul Starkey.
Other titles: Madåiòh li-nisåaʾ al-ʿåaʾilah. English
Description: Northampton, MA : Interlink Books, 2019.
Identifiers: LCCN 2018050160 | ISBN 9781623719845 (pbk. : alk. paper)
Classification: LCC PJ7862.H854 D3513 2019 | DDC 892.7/803—dc23
LC record available at https://lccn.loc.gov/2018050160

Printed and bound in the United States of America

To Mahdi, my fourteenth grandchild

1

Muhammad al-Asghar

We had to cancel our trip.

Sanaa grumbled and fell silent, as she usually did when something took her by surprise. Then she busied herself inspecting her clothes that she'd arranged in her suitcase, taking them out and putting them back into the wardrobe. With a mixture of regret and sense of loss, she looked at the bathing suit I'd bought her a few days earlier.

Sanaa had been keen to travel and visit Beirut again, a city famous for its warm climate, and its sea. I had visited it once before our wedding. Then after our wedding we spent ten days there. I continued to be impressed by it and wanted to go back again and again. I wanted us to be able to celebrate our twentieth wedding anniversary there, to renew our acquaintance with a city we loved and be reminded of the first days of our marriage. "How I long to visit the places where we were at that time!" Sanaa said.

We regarded the trips that some people here made as escapes from the reality that we lived in, or as acceptance of, and submission to, that reality, retreats to a private world in order to forget the world around us. When it became clear that things would remain as they were for no one knew how long, we realized it made no sense to just be unhappy, continuing to deny ourselves the simplest pleasures that could help us bear our burdens. We started to go out here and there, to enjoy ourselves a bit.

When we went to the Dead Sea together, I put on my swimsuit and swam in the water. Sanaa contented herself with her own personal ritual: she took off her shoes and lifted her dress above her knees, so that the water washed her legs and wetted the edge of her dress. When she met the women of the family one evening, she told them what she had done, to demonstrate that she did not respect the usual conventions of modesty. I sympathized with her, and she sympathized with me, because I carry the weight of the family on my shoulders, a weight that my father made me carry. Sanaa and I wanted to be free of the family and its cares, at least for a while.

My father named me Muhammad ibn Mannan al-'Abd al-Lat, known as al-Asghar (the Youngest), to distinguish me from two other brothers to whom my father gave the same name in honor of his own father, Sheikh Muhammad, who had an important position in the clan when our people lived in the desert. He called one of my brothers al-Kabir (the Elder) and the other one al-Saghir (the Younger). They went in totally opposite directions, and my father grumbled about them both. On several occasions, he announced before the sons of the family that he had put his trust in me. That he pinned his hopes on me to keep the various parts of the family together, to protect the women from any evil—especially after what had happened to my sister Falha and caused my father such grief—and do laudable deeds that would lift up the reputation of the al-'Abd al-Lat clan, which had spread its various branches, and scattered its sons, everywhere.

When I told him that I wanted to marry a divorcee three years older than myself, he just looked at me.

"You must be joking," he said.

"Not at all," I replied. "I'm not joking."

He took this decision of mine hard and almost withdrew his trust in me, lumping me in with my two brothers Muhammad al-Kabir and Muhammad al-Saghir, and with my brother Falihan, who'd committed several crimes. The year was 1962, and our general situation was not promising, political repression being at its height. He continued to give me one piece of advice after the other, stressing that I would be able to get a pretty virgin from Ra's al-Naba' or some other village around Jerusalem. But I would not be persuaded.

My mother was sympathetic towards me, in light of his opposition to my wishes.

Mother was obsessed with her shadow, sometimes following it and sometimes walking in front of it, in broad daylight. But this obsession didn't stop her from closely following the affairs of the family and interfering in its various trajectories. Despite her strong emotions, which sometimes made her angry, she had a good heart—unlike my father, who could be a little harsh. He continued to adopt a carrot-and-stick approach with me, but without success.

When Sanaa came to our house, she behaved with poise and tact, and spoke without any haughtiness. I had told my father that her former husband was her cousin, who was fifteen years older than her. They didn't have children because they had decided to wait for five years before having one. They lived together for three years but she couldn't tolerate his preoccupation with his business. She fled from him, and they agreed on a divorce. They went to court and stood before the judge. I was recording the case proceedings. Sanaa captured my heart from the start.

She came to our house, and my mother said she was a woman worthy of praise. Sanaa and her mother and father spent the whole day in Ra's al-Naba'. After she had left, my father said to me, "With God's blessing!"

That was twenty years ago.

Now, I could find no alternative but to cancel the trip, and I didn't know if we would be able to rearrange it in a few days' time. When we were getting ready to travel, my mother said that she had seen the family horse in a dream. The horse, which hadn't appeared in her dreams for some time, had shown up again. She said that it had neighed a lot, as if to warn us about the consequences of this trip.

Still, we were eager to go, despite the bullets that had been flying around there—sometimes more seriously—for seven years. We went to bed hoping that in the morning we would be able to cross the bridge to Amman, and from there board a plane for Beirut. But because air raids and chaos had engulfed the south of Lebanon, and were advancing towards Beirut like a flood, we couldn't travel.

I'm forty-two now. I've lived a life full of worries—family concerns, as well as concerns for Sanaa. This trip that we were hoping to make was in keeping with a ritual that we followed to relieve the family pressures on Sanaa. These pressures weren't in her hands, but she suffered from them, and as soon as they calmed down they'd flared up again. From time to time she would suggest to me that we separate. I wouldn't agree to a separation, though, because I loved her, and because my work in the sharia court had given me an aversion to divorce, the burden of which usually fell on the wives. I told her, "I won't separate from you, no matter how many burdens there are."

I worked in the sharia court in Jerusalem. I started there in 1958. My job wasn't of much significance, but for some time my relatives thought I was an important official when they saw me in my dark suit, blue tie over a white shirt, holding a black briefcase in which I kept papers and files. And I believed them. I believed I was an official of some importance, despite the fact that I was only a rather junior official in the hierarchy. My self-confidence grew, and I thought I would be able to please my father by fulfilling his wish to reunite the family.

I got the job at a time when posts weren't easy to come by. The credit for that goes to my father, who was able to take advantage of his relations with people who had come to prominence after the East Bank and West Bank were united, and who held posts in various government departments and institutions. He asked one of them to intervene to get me a post, and he found me a position as a clerk in the sharia court in Jerusalem, recording marriage contracts in a large register, as well as inheritance certificates and divorce papers. A lot of young women came to the court to register their marriages to young men, and divorcees also came to register second or third marriages to men who were older than they were, because they were in need of a man's protection. I saw so many examples of divorce for one reason or another, all sorts of reasons, in fact! As I look back over my time in the job, I can confidently say that these years definitely made an impression on me as they went by.

My brother Muhammad al-Saghir was always competing with my other brother, Muhammad al-Kabir, for influence over me, to define the direction I was taking with my life. Both of them tried to recruit me to their own views. I was wary, unenthusiastic about linking my life to convictions that might give me responsibilities I was incapable of fulfilling. Before I got my job, Muhammad al-Saghir told my father that he knew the director of the Religious Institute in Jerusalem, who was ready to accept me into the Institute, from which I would graduate as a sheikh, to lead people in prayers in the Haram al-Sharif. Although I was naturally religious, I hadn't thought of becoming a sheikh wearing a turban, so I wasn't excited about my brother's suggestion, and my father wasn't, either.

My father wanted to arrange a position for me that would provide me with a reasonable amount of money, of which he would take a share. He was no longer confident that he could rely on livestock, after investing his wealth in land he had bought here and there, and he was unwilling to accept any money from my brother Falihan because it was laundered. So I worked in the court. I wouldn't deny that my work there was out of tune with my dreams, but getting a regular salary at the end of each month makes you turn a blind eye. I consoled myself with the fact that I might be able to change careers and choose a job I liked better.

After completing a training course, in addition to my work in the court, I was given the job of writing marriage contracts outside the court. I became a religious registrar, a *ma'dhun*.

I would go to engagement and wedding parties, and sit between the families of the bride and bridegroom. I wrote the marriage contract and asked the bridegroom to put his hand on the hand of the bride's father, who had decided to give him his daughter in marriage. When the bridegroom had confirmed his acceptance, I would ask permission to go to the bride to hear her view. Preceded by her father, I would go into an adjoining room. One of her brothers would escort her from a crowd of women, and she would stand in front of me and give her agreement to the marriage, then return to the women.

I heard many girls give their assent to their marriages, only to discover later that their agreement had been the result of pressure from their father, or one of their brothers. Then the truth would emerge that the girl did not really want this husband, especially if it was a cousin or other relative, because she wanted to marry someone else. This would result in a wretched family life for her, which might well end in divorce.

But I would finish writing the contract, with the signatures of the parties and witnesses on it, and continue to sit with the guests. I could display no special knowledge on matters of religion. I would talk politics a bit and discuss the repressive atmosphere in which we lived. When we came under occupation, I would talk with others about the suffering of our people, but cautiously, for fear of agents who might report my conversation to their masters, in exchange for petty sums thrown in their direction, like a bone to a stray dog. I'd talk about the necessity of guarding the new generation from the decay of corruption.

Then the food would arrive—a *mansif*, made of rice, flat bread, meat and gravy. I'd ask for a spoon, which some tribespeople, accustomed to eating *mansif* with their hands, would find strange. They would roll a lump of rice and bread between their fingers and put it right into their mouths. I previously used to do the same, thinking it was a sign of good breeding, until a few days after our wedding Sanaa was appalled to see me stuffing rice in my mouth the same way, and asked me to eat with a spoon.

Whenever I was on my own, I remembered the hopes that my father had pinned on me: that I would be able to achieve something beneficial for the family and the clan. I would feel the weight of this hope, which meant closely following the personal secrets, dreams and fates of both the men and the women, among whom most prominently was my brother Falihan. My father gave him his name—Falihan ibn Mannan al-'Abd al-Lat—to perpetuate the memory of our uncle Falihan, who was killed in a war during the Ottoman sultanate. I told Falihan that we'd canceled the trip to Beirut—just as he expected, since his ear was always glued to the radio.

2

Falihan

My brother Muhammad al-Asghar believed that I was the obstacle standing in the way of the task my father had entrusted to him. I don't know whether he still holds to that belief or not…

Listening to the radio has become one of the few pleasures I indulge in during the day. In the evening, I spend two or three hours watching television—news, entertainment, a variety of songs sung by attractive female entertainers.

I love women's songs. When Samira Tawfiq appears on TV, I listen to her with my eyes glued to the mark near her nose, as she shakes her body gravely and rhythmically to the words of her song.

> *You with the white headdress,*
> *its color has changed on me,*
> *what shall I say, darling,*
> *my heart is on fire for you,*
> *what color is your heart for me?*

Whenever I hear it, the song takes me back and I remember when I was at the height of my powers in the prime of youth. If Rasmiyya makes a noise in the kitchen during the song, I get angry and shout, "I don't want to hear a sound!" Samira Tawfiq's singing transports me to delight. I remember how I used to listen to her singing coming from the radio and wish I could meet her and express my admiration. I saw her pictures in *al-Shabaka* magazine, through which I'd follow news about star singers and entertainers.

That was a long time ago, before the condition I ended up in. But even to this day, whenever I see Samira Tawfiq on the TV screen, I recall my earlier desire to get to know her. I try to bring her to life again, to take pleasure in the details of her appearance, before I wake up to reality and find consolation in Rasmiyya, who responds to my desires.

Rasmiyya is no longer young, but although she is in her fifties she has kept enough of her femininity to arouse me whenever I look at her body or embrace her. She sleeps beside me as though she were still in her twenties, and although I can no longer perform, I can put pleasure into her heart and feel enjoyment. Meanwhile, we recall together all the moments of intimacy there have been between us. I fell in love with Rasmiyya when she was engaged to her cousin. She didn't love him but agreed to the engagement to please her father. I will never forget the suffering I went through because of my love for her.

I sit in the wheelchair in the courtyard of my house, watching al-'Awda Camp, which crouches on the plain under the June sun, as I follow the news of the war in Lebanon—the war that has put an end to a trip by my brother Muhammad al-Asghar and his wife Sanaa. I realize that Omar, my brother Muhammad al-Kabir's son, is there in Beirut. Years have passed since the time when I and this brother of mine were at each other's throats. I am a supporter of any government supported by the royal palace, while he has always opposed them, except on one occasion: when that big symbol came to head what my brother regarded as a national government.

I cooperate with the occupation regime for fear of being detained, while Muhammad al-Kabir rejects it. I take one step at a time, while he carries a ladder openly. I have never been subject to detention, either under Jordanian or Israeli rule, while he has been suffering detention for years. I've kept to my moderate principles while he has kept to his, which I regard as extremist. He considered me a reactionary, may God forgive him. With time, our relationship improved, because he is my brother, and blood is always thicker than water.

Rasmiyya stands near me. She has finished sweeping the courtyard with a straw brush, sprinkling it with a little water to settle the dust and moderate the temperature in the summer heat. She leans her arm on my shoulder. How I like it when she stands there in this intimate way! She listens to the radio broadcasts about air raids on several locations in the south of Lebanon, and seems nervous as she pulls up the hem of her *thob* on both sides to fasten it under the waistband of her underwear. Since she stopped wearing long underwear, the white of her legs can be seen under her *thob*.

But she doesn't stay beside me for long. This always makes me cling to her and long for her to remain next to me. But she's restless, moving from one place to another, like a butterfly. She disappears inside for a bit, then comes back out carrying a morning coffee for her and me, with a hidden sadness in her eyes. "Tell me something new, Falihan," she says to me.

"There's no news except for the continuing raids and blood, Rasmiyya," I tell her.

We drink our coffee with the nervousness that has become our habit for much of the time.

When I snatched her from her fiancé, I didn't understand the enormity of what I had done. A moment of impetuosity and intrusiveness overcame me, and this moment reached its peak when Rasmiyya responded to me. I didn't mean to harm her family, who had been forced to leave their homes in the village of al-Wasima and come to this place near Jerusalem. They slept for weeks under trees before they got tents. It never occurred to me that I would see Rasmiyya and be attracted to her. I came with my first wife and my family and clan from the desert. I was living happily with my wife, and it never occurred to me that I would take a second wife, for my mother Mathila had suffered from her co-wives, as my father wanted to marry more than one woman. But Rasmiyya upset my calculations and set me on a path that I hadn't foreseen.

Despite the fact that I'd acquired sufficient education to qualify me to work as a clerk in a road-building workshop, or as a company employee, the desire to herd sheep and goats never left me. With sheep and goats, I could stay in touch with nature, which gave us the grasses that I awaited eagerly each year. I could earn a living from sheep and goats, and find in them a meaning for my life, even though later my sources of income became more diverse, as I amassed more wealth than any of my brothers or members of the al-'Abd al-Lat clan. Tending sheep brought me to Rasmiyya, or perhaps it made her appear on the horizon of my life.

But now I can't get out of this wheelchair—the reason being Sirhan, Rasmiyya's cousin, her fiancé, who tried to kill me years after all this happened. Sirhan said nothing until the right moment. But when he joined the resistance, he remembered the wound I had inflicted on him and opened fire on me. Although he didn't kill me, my legs were paralyzed when the bullet lodged in my pelvis. I also lost a function more important than my legs.

While we lived in the desert, my father would always say to anyone around, "This Falihan—I fear him, and I fear *for* him!"

He didn't pay me enough attention. He would put his hand on his heart, for fear of the mistakes I might make. He would really tell me off whenever someone came to inform him that I'd been loitering among the Rabahina campgrounds next to our clan. He found this strange, as he believed that I had abandoned my Qur'anic studies to tend sheep and goats. He would come looking for me and ask, "How can you leave the sheep and goats in empty ravines and come like a stray dog to hang around in our neighbors' camps?"

"Don't worry about the animals, Father," I would say to him. "There are three dogs with them to protect them." But he was never satisfied with that. So I would make up an excuse and say, "I forgot to take my provisions, and I'm on my way back to our campground to eat," but he still wouldn't believe me.

Here I was, spying on women who were busy either churning milk stored in goatskin jars to put on their thighs after lifting their *thobs*, or preparing food for their husbands and children, or bathing their children and washing their clothes, which they hung out in the sunshine on lines set up around the edges of the camp. How I wished I was a jar filled with milk, for a woman to put on her thigh, or a spoiled child for her to wash and cuddle in her arms. I found pleasure in watching the daily life of the women, who never stopped being busy from dawn until after sunset. I felt a tingling in my body as I saw some women in positions I would not have been able to capture if they had been aware of an adolescent watching them from a distance. I said to my father, "Marry me off to any of the girls of the clan!"

One night, the Rabahina clan had a wedding. I thought to myself that perhaps this would be the last wedding I'd see in the desert. Drought had given us no chance of remaining there, and my father talked of moving away, just as the Banu Hilal clan moved from Nejd to Tunisia in search of water and grazing.

I went to the evening wedding party. I stayed for a few minutes, watching the men lined up in the gathering, then slipped into where the women were singing and dancing.

From here to Safad there stretches a rope of desire,
from here to Safad God's command has been fulfilled,
they gave the beautiful girl to the handsome man,
God's command has been fulfilled.

I stood at a distance from the door of the house, and in the light from the lamp saw the girls prancing like thoroughbreds, their embroidered *thobs* hanging down over their bodies. I stayed there watching without anyone seeing me or turning me away. The women sang and danced as I watched them. One woman seemed to have been overcome by her exuberance, unable to contain her feelings, as she sang.

O plucker of pomegranates, what's wrong with my own?
Go away from the houses, and leave my pomegranates alone.

I couldn't wait. I went in, headed for the lamp, and blew it out. The singing and dancing stopped, and people began shouting. Then there was silence, as I said, "Girls, I've got something, I'm not saying what. Who wants it?" Someone said, "I want it," and the other girls laughed. "Get out, you devil, get out!" said one of them.

I hurried out and left the wedding. When the news reached the men of the clan, there was a great commotion, and their anger only subsided when my father pursued the matter in accordance with the established customs. I didn't escape his anger, as he struck me on the face, yelling, "What do you think you're playing at, you pimp?"

The following night, I sat like a wounded jackal, listening to the wedding songs in the distance, which went on for seven days and nights.

My father feared my doing anything that would expose him to harm. He was still unable to escape from the shame inflicted on him and the family by my sister Falha, who had eloped with her lover. He berated me, demanding that I go back to the grazing land. I was wary of his anger and went back, carrying my provisions of bread and cheese with me, and the epic of the Banu Hilal. I sympathized with 'Alya, whose husband Abu Zayd al-Hilali left her in her family camp, hoping that he would come back to her from his far-off place.

As my suspicious wanderings among the camps became more frequent, and I became involved in another scandal, my father found a fiancée for me from among the girls of the clan. I wished she had been called 'Alya, the beautiful woman that Abu Zayd al-Hilali had fallen in love with. When he resolved to marry her, his tribe refused to consent to his wish, for it did not allow its men to marry outside the tribe. But when Abu Zayd insisted on marrying his beloved, the clan gave in to him, and he married her. The name of my fiancée was Sheikha. I loved her name, which was just as exalted as the name of 'Alya. She was physically strong, not overly beautiful, but I loved her. When we moved from the desert to the heights above Jerusalem, Sheikha put up with all my moods. From the very beginning of her time with me, she observed how I strove to acquire money by any means, fair or foul. She was stunned when I fell in love with Rasmiyya, but didn't abandon me, despite the wrong I had done her.

Rasmiyya came to my attention when she traveled to the foot of the mountain. I realized that she had been torn from her home, from the place where she had been born and lived until she reached adolescence. She had been removed from the school where she used to take her lessons, then forced to leave her home and school, to leave her village with its trees and water, and the fields, plains and mountains that surrounded it. She had been made to come here against her will to live in a camp whose tents were alarmingly close together, so that there was no privacy and it was impossible to live a secure and honorable life. I watched her from a distance and pitied her, knowing how cruel time had been to her and her family. I started to sympathize with her, then began to see her as close to myself.

Now, here she is, sitting beside me in the courtyard of the house, drinking coffee with me and listening to the news of the catastrophe. She is preoccupied with my nephew Omar, just as she was twelve years ago, at the time of the slaughter in Amman. We were nervous at the time and prayed that the shooting would stop. Omar didn't come to any harm, and when the resistance left Amman and the forests of Jerash, he went with it to Beirut. Fazzaʿ, the son of my aunt Maʿzuza, who was a soldier in the army, wasn't injured either. But a lot of blood flowed that never should have.

Rasmiyya sits beside me. The whiteness of her legs reveals her femininity, which she has still retained despite the passing of the years.

I got to know her a few months after the 1948 disaster. I was tending my sheep and goats on our land, which my father had bought to the north of Jerusalem for us to use as pasture for our flocks. We later built houses on it, in one of which I lived with Rasmiyya, while others were occupied by my brothers and by our sons and daughters.

I saw Rasmiyya gathering wood with other girls from the camp. At first, I saw nothing to distinguish her from the others. I saw a lot of girls, looking like a herd of goats, with old shoes and torn sandals on their feet, and faded *thobs* covering their bodies. They had lifted the hems of their *thobs* to the left and right, and fastened them under the cloth belts that went around their hips, so that their long underwear—of a sort that our women in Raʾs al-Nabaʿ didn't usually wear, or even think of wearing—could be seen under their *thobs*. When I first saw them on the bodies of the girls in the camp, I was appalled.

What was the point of these trousers?

I saw the girls again in the spring at the foot of the mountain that ran parallel to our land as they gathered the mallow, thyme, and other herbs that were useful for cooking in times of hunger. I saw them in summer gathering firewood at the foot of the mountain, and wondered how the disaster had happened that had forced people to leave their homes and fields and orange groves.

My father used to sit in his guest room in Ra's al-Naba' before the disaster and say to those around him, "From the day I awoke to the world, this country has been tortured." Meanwhile, he would recall my brother Yusuf, who had emerged from prison in Acre, where he had said goodbye to five years of his young life. Yusuf once again joined the revolt led by 'Abd al-Qadir al-Husseini. When 'Abd al-Qadir was martyred in the battle of al-Qastal, my brother didn't despair. He continued the fight with the revolutionaries and was martyred in a confrontation defending Jerusalem.

His mother, Samiha, my father's fifth wife, insisted on his marrying when he came out of prison. Girls of the clan who were eager to get married would stand in his way to attract his attention in the hope that he would choose one of them to be his wife. They would send their little sisters to him with silk kerchiefs smelling of perfume, on which they had embroidered his name. They would come to our houses with their mothers, on the excuse that they wanted to visit his mother. But he paid them no attention, so much so that they believed he was no use to women. It seems he realized where life was taking him, and where his love for his country would take him. He chose to marry his country, and he had what he wanted. My father buried him, just as he had buried my brother Wattaf, killed before him by Jewish Agency employees.

I, Falihan ibn Mannan, thought, *it is better not to put myself in difficult situations. I want to live as long as possible, and harvest as many pleasures from this world as I can.* I continued to follow events in the country cautiously. When war broke out, my father continued to tell people in his guest room what he had seen and heard from the merchants of Jerusalem and his friends there. When he had tired of telling his news and stories, he would say, "The country has been lost and people displaced in every direction."

Rasmiyya and her family were among those who had been displaced. She would come to the foot of the mountain. I could see the bottom of her underwear, made of cheap material. But I was no longer revolted by her wearing the pants, as I had been before. Her pants had begun to pose a sort of challenge to me. The exaggerated way in which they covered her body began to tempt me to strip them from her, to see her hidden body and uncover its secrets.

One time I noticed that she was wearing gray-colored pants fastened around her legs. I realized that they were not her usual pants. She was also wearing a multicolored jacket over her *thob*. I saw other girls in the camp wearing brightly colored blouses, with scarves of cotton or wool tied around their necks. I later learned that these pants and other clothes were part of the consignments that came from overseas and were distributed to the camps for free.

I only saw Rasmiyya in the gray underwear three times. Perhaps she felt that her body was unduly constricted in them, or perhaps one of the village girls who hadn't experienced the tragedy of being a refugee had criticized her for them, and Rasmiyya hadn't liked it and had taken off her pants, once and for all.

When I approached her one morning, I didn't expect her to avoid me, but she did. I realized that she hadn't been thinking of me or paying me any attention. She was absorbed in picking the mallow at the foot of the mountain. She seemed to be avoiding me, though her breasts, which could be seen through her *thob*, presented me with an unexpected dilemma. I could see her long underwear, and I was overcome by a desire to uncover what was hidden. I felt a fever sweeping through my body. I called her.

"What's your name, girl?"

"Why do you ask?"

"Do you trust my words?"

She hesitated a little before answering.

"What words?"

"I'm sitting on one rock, and you're sitting on another."

I don't know why I resorted to this ritual, which we often used to use in the desert but abandoned when we started using written marriage contracts. I thought about the meaning of my words, but it seemed she hadn't understood what I meant. When she saw the lust in my eyes, she moved away.

"No, I don't want to."

I left her, unable to forget her.

Whenever I saw her, my blood would start to boil with desire for her. I would approach her using any excuse possible, stand close to her, take my reed flute from under my belt, and give myself up to playing tunes—sometimes dance tunes, other times sad ones. I would play the tune *Come on, come on, our loved ones went away without bidding us farewell.* Meanwhile, my eyes never left her as she continued to pluck the mallow and other herbs, listening to the tunes I was playing, while pretending not to.

I knew that Wadha would find another opportunity to ruin my reputation. I still recall her claim in front of the women of the family that I was a rival to her son Muhammad al-Asghar for the leadership of the family.

3

Muhammad al-Asghar
My mother, Wadha bint 'Abd al-Hadi, feared for me. She wanted me to be trusted by my father, against all rivals, like Falihan.

Wadha
How tired my head is and how many woes have I seen! My wish is for my son Muhammad al-Asghar to be well thought of by his father, Mannan Muhammad al-'Abd al-Lat, and so become the head of the family, and be able to fulfill the task that his father has entrusted to him. I say, and God is my provider, "Yes, Falihan, the son of my co-wife Mathila, is my son Muhammad al-Asghar's rival for the headship of the family."

And I say that Falihan listens to what his mother Mathila says. Mathila doesn't like me. She is jealous of me. She aimed to maintain her hold over Mannan's heart, but she failed. Mannan belongs to me alone, not to any of his other three wives. I am the youngest of his wives, the sixth in order of his wives. Mathila is twenty years older than me, and Safiyya and Samiha are also older than me, and Fatima and Watfa, may God have mercy on them, are dead. Mannan pays more attention to me than to Mathila, Safiyya or Safiha. I know how to keep him in my house, and I know how to keep him relaxed and contented. If Falihan wants to help his mother get the better of me, I say to him, "You will not succeed, Falihan."

From the day we left the desert, I have been saying to Mannan, "This Falihan of yours is untrustworthy." How many times have I said to my son Muhammad al-Asghar, "Do not go anywhere with Falihan. He might take you to graze the sheep and goats with him, and throw you into a deserted well, as Joseph's brothers did to Joseph."

How I feared for Muhammad when he was five years old. A woman visited us, with blue eyes and gappy teeth. She could bring down a bird in flight with her eyes. She saw him and said, "This boy's face is like the full moon in the sky." "Remember God," I said to her. "Say God's name and whatever God wills for him." She left me, damn her, and the boy started to cough, and rasp, and gasp for breath. As his cough got worse, I covered him in incense night and day.

A neighbor prescribed camel's milk. I milked a camel and gave the milk to him to drink. Then we took him to the doctor's. He gave him some medicine and advised us to let him stay in Jericho for a few weeks, so I took him there with Mannan. The weather was very cold in Ra's al-Naba'. We rented a room in Jericho and stayed there for two months. Our neighbor was a good-looking widow, from a good family, and I thought to myself that she might catch Mannan's eye. If I hadn't been scared something bad might happen, we would have stayed there longer, for the weather in Jericho was lovely and warm. We hoped he might get better, but he didn't.

We went back to the doctor and he wrote him a prescription and told us to take him to Jaffa, to breathe the sea air. So we took him to Jaffa and rented a room for two months. From the window of the room, we could see the British soldiers in jeeps and armored vehicles in the street. We could see the sea, the sea of Jaffa that stretched as far as the eye could see. I was afraid of it and said to myself, *How many secrets does this sea hold!* We could see the houses lined up next to each other—good God, how beautiful Jaffa was! But what annoyed me was that when the neighbors' daughter came down to the courtyard to play with Muhammad, her mother would call her and drag her away by the hand because she was afraid she might become infected. Despite this and everything else, we stayed in Jaffa for two months.

I said, "I'll try the medicine I learned from my mother, Marjana." I brought a piece of alum. The alum is a good woman, not to be afraid of. I put it on a piece of iron over the kerosene stove. It started to take on different shapes and colors. After a time, a picture of a jealous woman became visible. I saw her face and eyes. I brought a sewing needle and plucked out both her eyes, then recited the *shahada* and mentioned the name of God seven times. Afterwards, a neighbor prescribed a hyena's leg bone. I hunted for a bone and found one at a leather merchant's, then hung it on the boy's shoulder. We hoped he might get better, but he didn't.

Mahira, the wife of 'Abd al-Jabbar, the uncle of my husband Mannan, told me about a fortune-teller in Hebron. Mahira said, "Abd al-Jabbar started sleeping with his old wife two months ago and never leaves her."

We took the bus from Jerusalem to Hebron. We walked along a deserted street, and in the street, a strange thing happened to us. Merciful God, have mercy on us! A madman came up to us, with hair like that of a ghost. He was tall and thin. He saw us—Mahira and me—and took off his clothes so he was, damn him, just as his mother had given birth to him! God damn him! "By God, this is a devil," I said. I started reciting verses from the Qur'an, but he didn't stop. He looked at us and started to walk in our direction. I picked up stones, as did Mahira.

When he realized that we might break his head and draw blood, he was afraid. He turned his back on us immediately and ignored us as we walked towards the fortune-teller's house. The fortune-teller wrote a love amulet for Mahira, which she hid in the pillow that 'Abd al-Jabbar rested his head on, and wrote me an amulet against the cough, which I hung on Muhammad's shoulder, beside the hyena's leg bone. We hoped he might get better, but he didn't.

■

Muhammad al-Asghar

My mother Wadha gave birth to me in our house, which my father had built in Ra's al-Naba' a few years before I was born. I wasn't born in the desert and have never lived there. The al-'Abd al-Lat clan left the desert in the mid-1930s and set up their houses near Jerusalem. I know nothing about my family's life in the desert except what I have learned from my father and mother, and other relatives.

I was five when I contracted whooping cough, which frightened my mother and father. It lasted for three whole years. I remember my suffering with this cough as a vague dream, and I recall our stay in Jericho. I still remember the orange smells that the wind carried to the houses during the evening, and the tall mountain at the edge of the city, with a monastery on it, suspended in the belly of the mountain. I remember the woman who lived next door. She would come over from time to time to keep my mother company, helping her to cook and wash. She would open her arms to me, kissing me and hugging me to her chest, and my body would knock on her breasts. Then she would leave me to run in the courtyard under a sky covered in clouds. I will write all that down in my notebook, I will write down what my mother said in her very own way, her off-the-cuff manner, and sometimes I may intervene a little.

The only thing I remember of Jaffa is the sea. We used to go to the shore, and I would play with the sand as I breathed in the sea air, laden with varied smells. I was astonished at how blue the water was and by the waves, sometimes gentle, sometimes more violent. I would kick my foot against the waves as they subsided, then died away on the shore. I remember the neighbors' daughter who used to come down to the courtyard to play with me. I would clutch her hand and drag her towards me, then run and ask her to run with me. Then her mother would come with her hair falling over her face. She would fix me with strange looks, snatch her daughter from me, take her back to the house and shut the door, so that I was left alone outside, like a stray cat.

I know that my mother will return more than once to relate the details relevant to this illness. She will talk about her concern for me, about her readiness to go anywhere she might possibly find a cure for me, and about Jericho and Jaffa and her memories of them.

As was her habit, she would gossip during the evening about all sorts of subjects according to who was listening and how ready they were to listen to her. When she had stopped relating the events she had lived through in the desert or known from the mouths of others, she would return to Ra's al-Naba' and the details of her life there. She would recall her fear of the radio that the Mandate authorities had handed to my father and which rested on a table in the corner of the guest room. She believed the radio was haunted, so when she heard men's and women's voices emerging from inside of it, she would flare up and repeatedly call on God, asking him to preserve the al-'Abd al-Lat family from the evils of the creatures dwelling in the radio.

Once, when she was busy cleaning the guest room and getting the bedding ready for guests, she dared to approach the radio and turn it on. A vague, shaky sound came out and she became alarmed, reckoning that she must have awakened the creatures living there. She blamed herself and tried to stop the whispering but as soon as she touched the on button, voices poured out. She left the guest room but the voices continued to thunder, sometimes mingling together and sometimes on their own. My father wasn't at home, and my mother didn't dare go into the guest room again until one of the men of the family came and turned the radio off.

My mother recalls my brother Wattaf, who was martyred at the end of the thirties. His wife Mirwada was martyred after him. A band of Zionists came to Ra's al-Naba' under the cover of darkness and started to wander around the edges of the village, firing. After Wattaf was martyred, Mirwada hadn't left Ra's al-Naba' with her gypsy family—who moved to Jericho seeking warmth—but had stayed with her husband's family and spent a seven-year period of mourning for him. She left her house with stones in her hand. She believed she would be able to repeat what she had done when she smashed the head of one of the Jewish Agency's representatives, defending her husband, Wattaf. But he was killed in that incident, and Mirwada, before she could throw the stones as she had done before, was struck by a bullet fired by one of the band and killed.

My mother recalls the attack to which Mount Mukabbar was exposed in 1948. The Sawahira clans resisted it with their rifles and revolvers. A number of residents of Ra's al-Naba' came out to help, among them my father Mannan. He spent a considerable time cleaning and oiling his rifle. At other times, he would take shooting and target practice with a number of other men of his clan who had bought rifles for defending the homeland. "I was afraid for him when he went off to war," my mother said. "War is an evil woman, who swallows up men."

My father used up all the cartridges he had. After that, he put his rifle under his arm and returned home.

The events of that night became a subject of conversation that my mother never tired of repeating. She would choose a convenient time for it, for she couldn't bend our ears with her talk without some context, or an occasion that made it appropriate. Sometimes, she laid the groundwork for the Battle of the Mountain with events connected with what had happened in the country, so that everything came at the correct time and in the right place, and she would then continue, so that the conversation branched out and extended to several subjects. In any event, she was keen for my father to be there when she started her tale. He listened to her carefully, because he usually occupied a prominent place in her tales. She was like Sharazad tempting Shahriyar with her irresistible, never-ending stories.

She used to say that the band of men who came to Jerusalem with 'Umar ibn al-Khattab and were buried in Jabal al-Mukabbar at the end of their long lives, rose from their graves to fight the aggressors that night, and were seen by the men of the Sawahira who took part in the battle. My mother said, "They saw them appear in the form of white ghosts with swords in their hands." My father—without meaning to make people doubt my mother's words—said that he was busy firing and didn't have time to notice the band (may God be pleased with them!) in the fight.

She talked about her time with my father in the desert, and about their wedding, which was attended by the clansmen. She talked about his achievements and his generosity, and about problems he had encountered and emerged from safely. Sometimes she went too far in telling stories about him and revealed (perhaps intentionally) some of the secrets that he had shared with her. She talked, for example, about some of the women he had encountered in his life, and how they flirted with him in the hope that he would marry them. But he didn't pay them any attention because he had promised himself he wouldn't think of marrying any other woman after my mother.

She would tell her stories to us, grateful for my father's loyalty, while he felt satisfaction that she persuasively relayed his honorable attitudes to the younger generation, in a way that made them seem worth fixing in their minds and recording in their notebooks, as eloquent lessons for the sons of the family to be guided by.

As she told her stories, her conviction grew that she was taking on the role of storyteller at these evening get-togethers not simply because she was qualified and eager to do so, but also because she was continuing a tradition that my grandmother Subha—who had formed the memory of the clan over the years of her long life—had established during the clan's and family's evenings. My mother continued to remind us how my grandmother on her deathbed had entrusted her daughter with continuing to tell the stories after her, so she was embracing her task without hesitation, sometimes assuming the personality of the grandmother Subha while she was narrating. She did not do this so much when recalling that her own beauty was legendary among the al-'Abd al-Lat clan, but would go back to relying on the personality that had made my father devote himself to her to the exclusion of his other wives.

She would repeat to us my grandmother's stories out of reverence for her memory, though it was noticeable that she was not bound by the texts of the stories, which she varied, adding to and subtracting from them in accordance with her mood. She would say, "The story is a compliant female. A suitable addition to it does not detract from its value."

My relationship with Sanaa became one of her main interests, no less exciting than her interest in telling stories. A year after our marriage, she started feeling Sanaa's belly. She said she wanted to see my son racing with the other boys in the quarter. We talked about her recurring dream: She saw Sanaa walking proudly in the quarter, having turned into a chicken with lots of feathers, with seventeen chicks behind her, no more and no less. I smiled as I followed her dream, then asked her politely for a rest, saying that the child would come, and that all she had to do was to wait. She would purse her lips and say in a whisper, "Okay, God willing."

Sanaa said she wasn't in a hurry to have children. I had agreed with her to postpone it for five years. I didn't tell my mother or father about this decision, because from their point of view it was a disastrous decision, which threatened to weaken the al-'Abd al-Lat clan, perhaps expose it to the threat of annihilation. It was also in conflict with the task that my father had entrusted me with.

My father was concerned that I should have as many male children as possible, in line with an old desire that involved strengthening the clan so it could confront other clans in any dispute. He married six times, first to Mathila, then Safiyya, Samiha, Fatima, Watfa, and then to my mother Wadha, the youngest. He had eighteen sons and nine daughters. I told him, "Times have changed, Father." He would shake his head in sorrow and grief, and not insist too hard on his idea, as if he implicitly agreed with me that times had indeed changed, while he remained in limbo between a time that had passed (with all its pluses and minuses), and a present time that sometimes pleased and sometimes angered him.

I was in harmony with Sanaa, and she was in harmony with me. We lived our lives without any surprises. This harmony did not please my mother, since it was not resulting in children being born one after the other.

I recall one morning opening the court register in preparation for a sitting. As the man stood in front of him, the judge asked him, "What is your name?"

"Mu'tazz Ahmad Muhammad Yusuf," he replied.

"Age?"

"Forty."

"Employment?"

"Merchant."

"Place of residence?"

"Jerusalem."

"Wife's name?"

"Sanaa Rashid Muhammad Yusuf."

"How long have you been married?"

"Three years."

"Why do you want to divorce your wife?"

"She doesn't obey me."

"Explain, how doesn't she obey you?"

"She will only give me my marital rights after an almighty struggle."

"You mean, she does give you your rights in the end?"

"Sometimes yes, and sometimes no."

Then the judge asked the woman her name.

"Sanaa Rashid Muhammad Yusuf."

"Employment?"

"Bank clerk."

"Place of residence?"

"Jerusalem."

"Why do you want to divorce your husband?"

"I don't want him and he doesn't want me."

"Are you depriving him of his marital rights?"

"Sometimes."

"And the reason?"

"Incompatibility of temperament."

"Is there no chance of improving the relationship?"

"There is no chance."

"If I gave you time to reconsider the matter, would you agree?"

"There's no need for that."

I was recording every word that Sanaa said, looking at her admiringly as she stood before the judge. Her hair, which was almost golden, hung loosely over her shoulders, her wine-red dress flowed over her body. Underneath it could be seen two legs covered in soft stockings. I thought to myself, *My mother Wadha will heap blessings on me when I tell her that this woman entered my heart from the very first moment.*

While my mother turned a blind eye to Sanaa's extravagance and her slowness to conceive, she was recalling the misfortune of the co-wives, and their failure to show any grief over the death of my sister 'Aziza. She told her story, which she had often told in her evening gatherings, about the wife who didn't love her co-wife's dead daughter.

One morning she sent her a long way away to fetch a nigella plant, hoping she wouldn't come back. She put some food for her in a bag, without the girl knowing what sort of food it was. It was just bran and earth and fruit peelings. On the way, the girl passed a sheikh with a white beard, who was actually an angel. He stopped her and noticed the food.

"What's this, my girl?" he asked.

"This is bread," she replied without looking at the food.

"Bread? And what is this?" asked the angel.

"This is cheese."

"Cheese? And what is this?"

"This is lamb's meat."

"Lamb's meat? And where are you going?"

"To the land of plenty, to fetch a nigella plant."

The angel pointed out the way there for her, and she thanked him and went on her way. When she got hungry, she opened the bag and ate the tastiest of food. Then she continued on her way until she reached the land of plenty. The people of the country welcomed her and let her take the nigella plant, and she went back to her father's wife.

My father said, "Now for the surprise." He seemed eager to hear the rest of the story despite having heard it many times before. My mother continued.

The father's wife was jealous of her husband's daughter and decided to send her daughter to fetch the nigella plant. She filled the bag for her own daughter with the most delicious food, bade her farewell and prayed that she would return safe and sound. The girl went on her way and passed the sheikh with the white beard. He stopped her, looked at the food, and asked her: "What's this, my girl?"

"Shit," she replied haughtily.

"Shit?" he replied. "And what's this?"

"This is house waste."

"House waste?" he replied. "And what's this?"

"Cattle droppings," she replied.

"Cattle droppings? And where are you going?"

"To the land of the devils."

The girl proceeded along a rocky path. When she felt hungry she opened the bag, and found nothing in it fit for eating. She started to cry, when the sheikh with the white beard appeared to her. He said to her, "My girl, speak well, and avoid boasting and arrogance."

The girl felt sorry, and the angel helped her to return home. When her mother saw her in a state that no friend would like, she knew that she had received her punishment for wishing harm to her husband's daughter.

■

My mother finished the story and said, "The bird has flown, and may you have a nice evening!"

My father looked at her and sighed with satisfaction. She felt grateful because he paid attention to everything she said.

Before opening the gates of memory, she had a habit of putting her hand on her cheek. I would immediately feel less nervous because she would not be broaching the subject of Sanaa. She would pass quickly over our tragedies in her simple way, then move on to her favorite subject, the time that she had spent in the desert. She said that she was the daughter of a meek mother and a temperamental father who was extremely harsh towards his wife and children. She grew up in the desert and started to notice her shadow, which stayed with her on the plain and at the foot of the mountain, as if it was her brother. So as to forget the cruelty of her father, she occupied herself with her shadow and played a lot with it. She would stand on tiptoe, so that her shadow grew longer and longer. She would squat so that her shadow shrank, and she could touch it with her hands. She would lie down on the ground, so that her shadow was almost underneath her. She would laugh at it, and leave it asleep beside her, then get up and run off, and her shadow would run off with her.

She trained herself to get along with the people who lived there with her, who were only lively at night, and she prayed to God not to suffer any harm from them. She would start walking with her right foot rather than her left one so as not to disturb them. She wouldn't throw water at random wherever she found it, so that it wouldn't fall on their heads without their noticing, which might make them flare up with anger, then send one of them to take possession of her body so that she became mad. She never failed to carry out her duties towards her family. Meanwhile, her femininity blossomed as she ran over the plains and climbed the mountains. This was the best news she could give her mother, and her mother was delighted, for she realized that her journey through life had not been in vain.

My father loved my mother from the first glance, and she loved him. He became engaged to her and married her. Her mother was afraid for her because marriage carries responsibilities and she was only thirteen, and she thought of her as a child who was not yet ready for it. She said she was the youngest girl in the clan to have gotten married. I sometimes annoyed her, as she repeated the story of her marriage countless times, and said to her, "The Prophet Muhammad married Aisha, Abu Bakr's daughter, when she was nine." She asked forgiveness from God and seemed reluctant to delve into this matter. She said to me, "My son, this was only because of something that the Lord of Mankind wanted."

My mother moved from her home, where her family busied itself rearing cattle and cultivating the land, to the home of my father's family, which had similar interests. But my father's family had special rituals that were a little different from what she had been used to in her family home. There in her family home there were no secrets. Everything in the vast desert was open. Here in her husband's family there was an obvious desire to keep secrets as much as possible. If a boy or girl was sick, his or her illness was hushed up, and if a sheep from the flock died, it was buried secretly under cover of darkness, for fear of men or women gloating over their misfortune. Perhaps the scandal of Falha, which the family couldn't keep secret, was one of the reasons for this eagerness to hush things up. Her husband's family also had memories of grandfather 'Abd Allah's horse, whose ghost continued to visit some of the women of the family and keep them awake after its rider had been killed, as if it was grieving for its betrayed rider, or was not content with the situation of the al-'Abd al-Lat clan, split up and humiliated.

When the 1948 disaster unfolded, my mother was living with my father in Ra's al-Naba', with only faint memories of the desert left in her head.

4

Muhammad al-Asghar

In 1948 I was just beginning to become conscious of life. I was only eight, but my mother never stopped proudly repeating, "You're a man now." She seemed to be hurrying time along, impatient with waiting. I observed my mother's daily life intimately. My father was always busy with family and clan affairs, and was away from home almost all day, or else busy meeting with men in the guest room. From time to time I would go to the guest room, then come back to my mother, feeling safe beside her. When she was in a bad temper or preoccupied, gossiping with a neighbor, she would send me away and I'd leave without a fuss.

My mother lowered the seven flags she had raised over the roof of the house when I'd recovered from whooping cough. She was forced to lower them because she couldn't tolerate the slightest disturbance. I couldn't comprehend everything that was going on around me at the time but understood that there was killing and bloodshed, and that Palestinians were being turned into refugees. I listened to stories told by people I knew and by others I was meeting for the first time before they disappeared. Things were confusing, and life no longer went along on its usual course.

Whenever I had the chance, I would listen to what people were saying in my father's guest room. They came to hear news on the only radio that the al-'Abd al-Lat clan possessed, and to find out what was happening—and had happened—in the country, from eyewitnesses who were visiting as guests of my father. I heard about the atrocities committed against people by the Zionist gangs, about the massacre of Deir Yassin, in which the bellies of pregnant women were slit open, about the massacre of al-Dawayma, in which a hundred and seventy children, among others, were killed and women were raped, and about their forced expulsion from their homes. I heard the sound of bombs over Jerusalem, and I was afraid.

■

Najma, the wife of my uncle 'Abd al-Wadud, worked in the house of Hanna, a bank employee, and his wife 'Afifa. The house was in the Talibiyya Quarter. It was in Talibiyya and al-Qatmun that the well-heeled elite Jerusalemites—merchants, intellectuals—lived. Every morning, Najma left her house in the Maghrebi Quarter of Old Jerusalem and made for the Talibiyya Quarter to clean Hanna's house and to cook for him, for 'Afifa, who worked as a teacher, and for their children, who came home from school in the afternoon.

Najma was content with her life as a servant to Hanna and 'Afifa, and was convinced that she had done the right thing when she left Ra's al-Naba' to live in the city. But the family thought otherwise, especially when Najma took off her long *thob* and put on a dress. My brother Muhammad al-Saghir talked about her with loathing and called her a slut. "Najma is a respectable woman," my mother replied. "She is a perfectly well brought-up lady." Some women of the family envied her for her beauty, which the tyranny of time had diminished only a little.

As danger approached the Talibiyya Quarter, Najma was afraid of the noise of the bombs and gunfire, and anticipated that the simple glory she had created through her efforts and hard work was about to collapse. She was sorry for herself, and for Hanna and 'Afifa, who would have nowhere to go if they were forced to leave the house they had lived in for so many years.

Many families left because of the repeated attacks on neighboring quarters. It seemed that the next attack would be on the Talibiyya Quarter itself. People abandoned their homes, furniture, and everything else they owned, and left. They left their family photos on the walls of their homes, left suits, dresses, coats and shirts in the cupboards, books on the shelves, roses and other plants in their china pots. They left their bedrooms with the curtains lowered, and they departed, taking with them only a few belongings and an excess of memories. Maryam, the wife of my brother Muhammad al-Kabir, would tell how the house of the teacher and educator Khalil al-Sakakini, which was in the al-Qatmun Quarter, was seized, with all his reference books.

Najma suggested to Hanna and 'Afifa that they and their children stay in her house in the Maghrebi Quarter until the problem was resolved, although she believed that the outcome would involve massive damage. Despite that, she tried to minimize the blow of the tragedy for them. "God willing, things will calm down and people will come back to resume their normal lives."

They smiled sadly as they listened to what Najma said, at the same time continuing to choose which belongings to take with them.

After the fall of the western part of Jerusalem, Hanna and ʿAfifa and their children left their house in the Talibiyya Quarter. Najma went back to the Maghrebi Quarter, whose low houses had not escaped the bombing. She stubbornly remained in her house, with her husband ʿAbd al-Wadud, while the fighting in Jerusalem was at its fiercest.

Their daughter, Nawal, worked as a teacher in a school in the city. She had three sons with her husband, who worked as a dentist. She seldom visited Raʾs al-Nabaʿ. "Why should I visit when the people there still have a primitive desert mentality and do nothing but gossip?" she'd complain.

Nawal avoided the clanswomen and they avoided her, accusing her of arrogance. When they held get-togethers in the morning or evening, they found her absence a subject ripe for discussion. They would dissect her from tip to toe, and accuse her of having a relationship with the preacher ʿAbd al-Qadir, from whom she'd learned to read and write. One of them claimed that he played with her breasts. My mother shook her necklace, invoking the name of God seven times, and asked the clanswomen to speak properly and refrain from using bad language about respectable women. But they wouldn't desist or stop the winks and nudges; in fact, they went on with them until the sun was in the middle of the sky, or a shy moon appeared from behind the horizon.

My father put up with the gossip about Nawal among the clan and the family in Raʾs al-Nabaʿ, and never ceased boasting to his merchant friends in Jerusalem that his niece was married to a dentist.

Father had asked for her hand for my brother Adham before she married the dentist, but she wouldn't accept Adham as a husband. Adham was shocked, which left an obvious impression on him and set him on a path that was not free of surprises. My father put up with the snub, just as he had with others. I saw in all this a burden to be added to my other burdens connected to holding the family together, despite the fact that all this had happened years ago. But its effects had lasted to the present day, eating into the body of the family, never leaving it alone.

Nawal paid no attention to Adham. She forgot him at once and continued to live outside the wall in the eastern part of Jerusalem. My uncle 'Abd al-Wadud and Najma continued to live in the Maghrebi Quarter near the wall. My uncle and his wife loved this quarter for the warm relations that had sprung up between neighbors, which showed that Jerusalem had embraced a diversity of ethnicities. The Maghariba had come there from North Africa to fight with Salah al-Din al-Ayyubi against the Europeans and to liberate Jerusalem from their raids. They came there as pilgrims to the al-Aqsa Mosque and took up residence there, then became proper Jerusalemites. 'Abd al-Wadud had Maghrebi friends in the quarter, and Najma was happy to live there. Luckily, her house was not exposed to any harm or hit by the missiles that rained down on the quarter from the west.

Despite that, Najma felt frustrated. She felt that what had happened was too much for her to absorb. She cursed the strangers who had taken over her life and made her feel anxious about her future and the future of the country. She often regretted leaving the Talibiyya Quarter and the pleasant life there. She remembered Hanna and 'Afifa and the children, and wondered where they were living now. She said, "I bet they've gone across the river."

More than once she tried to take the path she had used to walk every morning to the Talibiyya Quarter, but she came up against barbed wire and the border zone that separated East from West Jerusalem and had to return to where she had come from. She told my uncle 'Abd al-Wadud what she was doing, and he'd warn her, "Be careful, Najma, they'll kill you!"

Then she found out that Hanna and 'Afifa had come back from Amman, after the truce and the end of the fighting and the loss of most of Palestine, and had rented a house in the Sheikh Jarrah Quarter. She learned this by chance as she was going to the baths. There she met 'Afifa, whom she embraced with warmth and love. She went back to working in her house as she had done before, with a lump in her throat that never left her, though she hid it and never let it become apparent.

A lump stayed in my father's throat as well, for many years. I asked him to go easy on himself, because the family's woes were too many to be counted. This was some years after Nawal had refused to marry Adham. My father was still weighed down by cares. Adham opened his heart to me and told me everything. I liked the fact that Adham trusted me but was still worried about my father.

"Look after your health, Father," I said to him. But he didn't like me giving him advice when he was used to giving me advice. My mother said, "Better to leave your father to do as he wants."

"I want him to calm down."

"I know what you want, my son, and I know what your father is like. He doesn't like anyone giving him advice as if he were a small child."

"I haven't been treating him like a child, even though he sometimes behaves like one as he gets older."

"Quiet, child, in case he hears you."

So I said to him, "Father, don't blame me if I have done wrong."

"I am not angry with you, Muhammad, my son," he replied.

I thanked him, and we sat and made conversation in the guest room. My mother left us, repeating her usual pronouncement, "I'm going to bed to rest my bones."

■

In the midst of all these ups and downs, my aunt Ma'zuza married. She had waited a long time. No suitor had appeared by the end of her period of mourning for her beloved Harran ibn Hafiza. My mother sighed, for she was fond of Ma'zuza and wished that a decent man would come for her.

A decent man appeared with the bunch of Jordanian troops who defended Old Jerusalem in 1948. The soldier, Sayil, had a shoulder wound. He was treated in a field hospital, but his wound took time to heal. My brother Youssef got to know him during the fighting. He brought him to our house in Ra's al-Naba' to convalesce, in the course of which he got to know my aunt Ma'zuza. They fell in love with each other, though she was twelve years older than him. She was forty-two years old, but he was attracted to her.

Mathila, my father's wife, told how Ma'zuza used to bring him breakfast herself. She said she heard Ma'zuza cooing from inside the room, the sort of noise that divulged her passion, and it stayed with her. Then she saw her near Sayil, washing his wound with soap and water, and dressing it with a clean white bandage.

Sayil asked my father Mannan for her hand. He promised he wouldn't neglect her and that she would live with him like a queen. He said to my father, "I will make Ma'zuza the apple of my eye, Uncle." The wedding took place with no singing or chanting, because Palestine was falling into enemy hands. Sayil married her and stayed in Ra's al-Naba' for some weeks. Mathila said—and her words were repeated by the other clanswomen—"Her husband's smell has given Ma'zuza back her spirit." She also said, "Her belly has opened out, her cheeks are rosy, and she seems younger than she really is."

Sayil left Ra's al-Naba', taking my aunt Ma'zuza with him to Madaba, where they lived for several years near her co-wife, Sayil's first wife. How happy we were when we visited her in her home there and listened to her talking in the distinctive accent of the Jordanian women of Madaba!

My brother Muhammad al-Kabir had not yet been exposed to government violence. I viewed him with curiosity. At times I admired him and his ideas, and at others I was wary of him. He continued to work in the Garden of the Holy Sepulchre, with Maryam, who became his wife. The city, with its Muslims and Christians, was recovering from the blow that had struck it and was regaining its ability to challenge and survive.

My brother lived with his wife in a house they rented outside the city wall. It was said that he had gone with her to

Greece, where they married in the Orthodox Church, using different rites from those followed here in Jerusalem. Another story was that they had married in the Greek Orthodox Church of the Annunciation in Nazareth. Other people said that a leader of the Communist Party had drawn up a marriage contract for them in his own hand, signed by himself and two witnesses, and that was how they were married. So far as I know, no one asked for any clarification from my brother of the details of what had happened, and he did not provide any clarification to anyone. He simply said, "The important thing is that we—Maryam and I—agreed to marry."

My father wasn't angry that my brother had married Maryam. On the contrary, he wished her all blessings and happiness for having accepted Muhammad as a husband, when he had previously been wild and unsettled.

My mother was kind to him and admired his thick mustache, which he had grown after a trip he had made to Russia with Maryam. My mother knew that the leader of that country was named Stalin, that he had a thick mustache, and that supporters of the Soviet Union let their mustaches grow to look like his.

But it wasn't my brother's mustache that was the problem, and it wasn't my brother and his wife that were the problem. As the one charged with keeping the family united, I have to acknowledge that the headache experienced by my father and uncles, and other members of the family and clan, on account of my sister Falha.

Falha came back after being away for some time. She had fled from our house in the desert with her lover Nu'man. I saw her when she finally came to Ra's al-Naba' with her brother Falihan, who had found her again. He said:

I noticed a woman, among the women and girls of the camp, who did not hide her face from me. I said to myself, *This woman is like my sister Falha. But my sister died a long time ago—my father's uncle slaughtered her after coming across her in a village*!

I started to watch her. Then I forgot about her. She always looked down at the ground. One night I dreamed that I had met her and asked her, "Are you my sister Falha?" She replied, "Yes." I said, " But 'Abd al-Jabbar killed you at Shubriyya."

Before she could answer me, I woke up wondering if I should have asked that woman in the camp who she was.

I took the animals to pasture and waited until the women and girls of the camp came. I looked carefully at the first group, and she wasn't among them. I looked carefully at the second group and saw her. I went up to her.

When she saw me, she looked at my face and I looked at hers. She recognized me, and I recognized her. "Falha!" I exclaimed anxiously. "Falihan!" she cried in a passionate voice. She kissed me on my cheek and forehead. "I saw you looking after your animals," she said, "but paid you no attention and did not look at you. But when you came up to me, I recognized you."

When I saw her with her head covered with a kerchief, wearing a *thob* with long pants underneath it, it never occurred to me that this was my sister Falha.

She said, "I was living with my husband Nu'man in his village, Wasmiyya. Nu'man and I, his family, and all the people of Wasmiyya, had to flee because of the attacks and the shooting and killing."

When she came back with her brother, she didn't recognize me because I hadn't been born when she left. Falihan said, "I can forgive her for her lapse, because my father was to blame at the time." He added, "Nu'man came to ask for her hand and marry her in accordance with the custom of God and his Prophet, but Father refused the sweet seller's request."

My mother Wadha told my father, "Mannan, since Falha is happy to be his wife, why do you reject him?" He answered her, "Wadha, you don't know anything about these things, so you'd better be quiet." She said she had kept quiet and that she was no longer sure it was a man who came to ask for Falha's hand in marriage, but a jinn who came in the guise of a man and then lured her into going off somewhere with him.

My brother Falihan said that his mother Mathila wanted Falha to marry the sweet seller, but she had gone on pilgrimage, so the matter remained unresolved. The solution came from Falha. When Father rejected her wishes, she left with her lover. Although Falha landed Father in trouble, it was a problem he had created himself.

Falihan brought her to Ra's al-Naba' because he wanted to restore relations that had been severed between us, and she stayed in our house for some time. Then Falihan traveled with her back to the camp where she lived with her husband Nu'man.

Over time, Falihan's love for Rasmiyya, whose family was displaced, continued to grow, and gradually she warmed to him.

5

Falihan

She said she was engaged to her cousin and would be married in a matter of months. I told her I loved her and that I loved her long underwear. Then I urged her to leave him. She said she didn't love him and didn't hate him either. I told her I was ready to marry her, she just had to announce her refusal to accept him. She said she had compared the two of us and found me closer to her heart than he was. She declared that she had accepted me as a husband. We were alone in the desert that day. I embraced her, and she showed only a faint resistance. I was not deterred. I stretched her out on the grass, took off her underwear, drew her *thob* up to expose her pale skin, then forgot everything. My eyes clouded over, and when I opened them, the grass around us was so much greener!

Afterwards, she was afraid and believed I wouldn't keep my promise and marry her, but I remained faithful to her. She had to take the first step. She said, "I can no longer taste sleep."

I agreed with her that she should publicly reject her fiancé. She said, "When I announced my refusal, my father, mother and brothers were angry with me, and so was my fiancé."

I discussed the next step with her, and we agreed that she should leave home and stay temporarily in Sheikh Za'al's house, the head of the Muza'ila clan. She left camp secretly. She said, "I stayed for some weeks in the sheikh's house, and he sent three members of his clan to my family to tell them that I was loved and honored in his house, and that I was safe and secure there."

As if to make me bear responsibility for what had happened to her, and recall what we had experienced together, she said, "My father refused, but later submitted to reality, though he didn't agree to my returning to the camp. He left me to become engaged and to marry away from my family home, though he agreed that my mother and sister should attend my engagement and wedding parties."

Her cousin canceled the engagement, and my father sought her hand for me from Sheikh Za'al. I married her after an engagement of a few weeks.

The women sang on the wedding nights and danced as if they were shaking from their bodies the dust of long days of bloated monotony, as well as suffering and sorrow. Many of the men of our clan, even the more elderly, had no hesitation in joining the party, while the younger ones enthusiastically danced the dabka to the strains of the *shabbaba* or the flute.

I was happy because I was going to marry Rasmiyya, who was more beautiful than my first wife. I tried to make Sheikha happy with sweet words and new clothes. I danced the dabka and played the *shabbaba* on my wedding nights, singing happily and uninhibitedly.

On the wedding night itself, I was alone with my bride and thought to myself that I would see her body and get to know its youthful details legitimately. I would find out the effect of the wound that I inflicted on her with her consent (or rather, with only a little resistance), in a moment of emotion that made her unable to control herself, though she later blamed herself and regretted it, she told me.

I approached her, and she looked towards me but said nothing. I tried to embrace her but she did not respond to me. She said she was tired and that I had to give her a night or two's rest. She didn't give me a chance to reply to her or carry on talking in the hope that she might respond to my wishes. I realized that I was in front of a different woman.

She took out a knife from her box of clothes, nicked her arm lightly to make the blood flow, then caught it in a white handkerchief that she took out from under her sleeve. She let it bleed until the spot of blood had spread over the handkerchief. Then she asked me to go out to the waiting women.

The shrieks rang out. Rasmiyya wept, then wiped away her tears before her mother could come in to her with some other women, to congratulate her on the legal act, which had taken place without any delay.

I tried to approach her bed on the second and third nights but was met only with rejection and obstruction. I thought, perhaps she was having her period and was embarrassed to tell me. Perhaps she was feeling guilty because of what took place between us, and because I exposed her to a rift with her family. I told her I understood what she was suffering, but that it would would all go away soon, and relations with her family would return to what they were before.

But her father, brothers and other family members did not forgive her. She said she cried the whole of the last night she spent in Sheikh Za'al's house, for she realized that she would not be moving to her marital home from her father's house, but from the house of a man who had received guarantees from her family that they would not expose her to any harm. She said, "I hated myself for bringing on my family this new problem, as if the problems they had had since they were made to leave the country weren't enough."

She said that when she recalled what had happened between the two of us at the foot of the mountain, her eyes were covered in darkness, and she had evil feelings. She didn't know how these feelings had formed inside her, or how she could get rid of them so as to put her life back on an even keel.

I carried on treating her gently and speaking kindly to her, but she didn't reciprocate or respond to me at all. Although I am known for my harsh nature, I was patient and put up with her rejection, until she started to emerge from the mood that had taken over her life.

On the seventh night, she started to get ready to wash herself. I could see her in the dim light as I lay in bed. She set the round metal basin in the corner of the room, with a pitcher full of warm water beside it, a loofa, a piece of soap, and a bowl for pouring the water. She took off her clothes, and I could see her body in the slightly murky corner as she stood in the middle of the basin, like a beam of light. She bent down and poured the bowl of water over her hair, then washed her hair with soap. I thought of getting up from the bed to pour the water over her body but was afraid she would push me away, so I preferred to let the scene work itself out in the way that she intended. Her hair hung down over her shoulders and chest; she pushed it aside to wash her shoulders and chest, then washed her belly, her back, her thighs and legs. The soap left a thick foam at the folds of her body.

She rinsed herself with water, and the remains of soap disappeared. She tied her hair up on her head. Once again I was about to get up from the bed to dry her body with a blue towel near me, but I preferred to wait, so as not to spoil the end of the scene, which was arousing in me some expectations.

"Hand me the towel," she said. I leaped out of bed and took hold of the towel. I started to dry her body gently and breathlessly. She embraced me in her arms as I was busy drying her body. I carried her in my arms to the bed. "Do you love me?" she asked. "Do you doubt it?" I asked her, panting from the strength of my emotions.

She didn't reply to me but when she kissed my nose and brow I knew the answer.

I'd asked her when she went with her mother to the market to buy clothes for the wedding, not to wear long underwear, but to wear short pants instead, as was the fashion in Ra's al-Naba'. She hesitated and said she was used to the other sort of pants. She said she'd tried to wear short pants before, and felt naked, with nothing to cover her body. She said her mother might object, and think it wanton and immoral.

I suggested to her that she buy a dozen short pants to wear under the long pants. She smiled and found the suggestion amusing. She said she would do that, so I gave her enough money, and she went to the market with her mother and sister. They spent a whole day in Jerusalem, shopping.

Some months went by after our wedding before Rasmiyya was convinced that she should finally dispense with her long underwear. Whenever she walked among houses in Ra's al-Naba' belonging to the clan or walked past a shop with men gathered at the entrance, she had felt embarrassed, as though someone might ask, How can you leave your house without pants? She complained to me about this. I said to her, "You'll get used to it in time, just like the other women of the clan."

Heaping blame on herself, she said, "Goodness, I mean, am I supposed to turn this subject into the story of Abu Zayd al-Hilali?"

I laughed and said, "Yes, but that was a long time ago."

She laughed and tried to joke with me, to prove to me that she was no longer embarrassed, and lifted her *thob* up until you could see the whiteness of her legs.

Wadha, my father's wife, didn't like what I had done. She didn't like it that I had appropriated someone else's fiancée, as if I despised him or thought him a weakling. She sometimes accused me of trying to mix milk with water, but I took no notice of her. But I felt sorry when I saw how, without intending to, I had brought harm to good people who had lost their land and their homes and been expelled from them. I felt even more sorry when I observed how Rasmiyya's father had been inspired to act in a measured way by a desire to let bygones be bygones and not resort to harsh measures that might cause even more grief.

Rasmiyya said, "I won't cause you any trouble, Falihan."

After I'd married her I became certain of that and said to her, "Your face brings me goodness and blessings, Rasmiyya."

I had managed to secure a livelihood, and my relationship with Sheikh Za'al had become firmer after Rasmiyya had taken up residence in his house. I used to meet him with his men who came to sell their sheep and goats in the official market near the Jerusalem wall.

■

We got to know each other for the first time in the market. After we'd sold our livestock, I invited them to sit in Muna's café at the beginning of Wad Street, so we went there and drank coffee. Four men were there. The oldest one, who was the clan sheikh, said he knew me from before. He knew that I belonged to a clan that had a good reputation among the clans, and had heard only good things about my father Mannan, the head of the al-'Abd al-Lat clan. I thanked him for what he had said and continued to listen to him. He said he wanted to get to know me and the other members of my clan. So he invited me to take lunch in his house, and extended a welcome to me and any of my relatives I might take with me.

After my father declined the invitation for personal reasons, I headed for the Maza'ila camp, which was situated on the road between Jerusalem and Jericho, with three of my closest relatives. We sat in the house, sleeves rolled up, with sweet breezes blowing onto us. Sheikh Za'al welcomed us every two or three minutes, then ordered a young man to bring us bitter coffee. We observed how the members of the sheikh's clan were ready to pick up any hint from him and turn it into a generous action.

I was delighted by the warm hospitality we received from the sheikh and the members of his clan, and I invited him and any relatives he would like to bring with him to take lunch in our house in Ra's al-Naba'. The sheikh accepted the invitation and came with five members of his clan. I met them with my father Mannan and a number of members of the al-'Abd al-Lat clan, and we slaughtered some animals and gave the guests a feast.

Two weeks after my wedding to Rasmiyya, we met in Muna's café, and I realized that the sheikh had something to say. He told me that he and some of his fellow clansmen had a business which gave them a good income and that they would like me to cooperate with them if I wanted to make some money. As soon as I heard these words, I said, "I am with you completely."

"And are you ready to put up with difficulties?" the sheikh asked.

"I am your brother, and I will not let you down."

"The work may involve murder, and may involve impris-onment," the sheikh went on. "Governments have no mercy in this sort of thing."

"I am your brother and am not afraid of death," I replied. "Don't you trust me?"

"Yes, of course I trust you," he replied, stroking his mustaches.

We shook hands and made a pledge to be true to each other. He asked me to select a group of my own clansmen to guard the goods from raids by other clans when the caravan passed through their territory and to ensure its safe passage to the southern border. I told him I was completely ready to undertake the task. I made him even more enthusiastic when I told him that I could guarantee shipments of goods to the enemy state that had recently come into existence, and which had a border with Ra's al-Naba'. Sheikh Za'al expressed his pleasure at this new opening for a different sort of income.

I grew rich from the hashish trade, and I bought gold bracelets, rings and necklaces for Rasmiyya, Sheikha and my mother Mathila. For my father I bought striped abayas. When he learned the source of my wealth, he disapproved of it but he didn't take a harsh line with me. He contented himself with refusing to accept any clothes or money from me, for fear of God's wrath. His attitude did not deter me from doing what I was doing, and I persevered with my money making.

I acquired a position of authority in the clan, with many acquaintances in Jerusalem and other cities, as well as close friendships with officials in Amman, whom I showered with presents and gave banquets for. The money was not to be made easily. Together with my companions, I fought several battles on dark nights with highwaymen and greedy tribesmen who held us up on our way to deliver goods to our agents in the desert.

We gave money to some tribal sheikhs so that they would not hold us up, and clashed with others who were satisfied with nothing less than seizing our goods. We drew our rifles and opened fire on them, and they would return fire. Both we and they suffered losses, then things would go back to their normal state.

Sometimes, we would send a quantity of goods to the enemy state. At a distance from the border, there was a guard post manned with soldiers. Once, one of them saw me grazing my animals in no-man's land. The plentiful grass had tempted me to enter the area with no regard for the consequences, so I left my animals to go there to graze. He called to me in Arabic with an Iraqi accent and ordered me to come over, which I did. Then he asked me to sell him a sheep, which he paid for in dollars. After that, I started to sell him a sheep from time to time. We agreed on a certain signal when his turn came to be on guard duty.

I sold him sugar, tea, rice, cigarettes and cloth. Later I started to sell him pieces of hashish. This didn't last long, for I made an unforeseen mistake, thinking that the Iraqi Jew would be in the guard post, when I discovered that I had gotten the timing wrong and a soldier opened fire on me, and I almost lost my life. After that, I never went near the border area.

Our trade across the desert continued, however, and the money began to pile up in my pockets. I spent whatever I liked, however I liked, with banquets that the Ra's al-Naba' and other clans talked about, as well as people in Jerusalem and the surrounding villages

Once, in 1953, I invited General Glubb Pasha, who was nicknamed Abu Hanik, to take lunch in my house in Ra's al-Naba'. My fellow clansmen made a guard of honor with me. They killed some animals, lit fires, and the women of the clan soaked the frozen *laban*, without which lamb's meat does not taste good. The pots were filled with *laban* and with meat cut into medium-sized pieces, and the flags of the kingdom were raised over the roof and wall of my house. My father felt proud of me, despite knowing where the money had come from. He was surprised that I was important enough to be able to invite the head of the Jordanian army to eat lunch in my house. I was swaggering about in the courtyard, where dozens of tribal no-tables and fellow clansmen were lined up, awaiting the arrival of the leader and his henchmen. After a long wait, he arrived in a cavalcade of army vehicles. He got out of one of them, surrounded by guards bristling with weapons. The women of the clan ululated and sang to greet the important guest. I was the first person to greet him. I took him in my arms and kissed him on both cheeks, and didn't try to avoid his small chin, which had been disfigured by a bullet some time ago. My father, Mannan, greeted him, but for some reason didn't kiss him on his cheeks.

The leader greeted a number of other tribal notables with a humility that people were unable to explain. He took off his shoes, sat on the bedding and drank three servings of bitter coffee, then shook his cup to indicate that he had had enough. He ate our *mansif* exactly as we clansmen do, that is, directly with his hand, fashioning balls held together with rice and pieces of dry bread. My father tried to explain his humility and precise observance of our customs, commenting, "This is the policy of the British—they are slippery like no one else." My uncle 'Abbas backed him up. "That's right, he pretends to be one of us, like us in everything, and then we discover that he's digging a hole for us God only knows how deep! If you'd asked me," he went on, "I'd have advised you not to ask this man to your house."

I was cross with my uncle 'Abbas for saying that, for he had shut up his shop in the city before lunchtime and had come to show me respect, imagining that we were still living in the desert, although he had become a city dweller. He should have been the most understanding about what I was trying to do. But my uncle 'Abbas, like my father Mannan, had his own private concerns. He would accept the invitation to lunch and say hello to Glubb Pasha, then the next day boast in front of his merchant neighbors that Abu Hanik had been a guest of the al-'Abd al-Lat clan. The merchants would gape in astonishment at this bombshell, but my uncle would cut off any of them he thought fit to by saying, "This man works in the service of his country, Britain, which colonized us." Then he would say what he had said to me after the meal. I imagined this scene, then said to him, visibly agitated, "Uncle, spare yourself the advice. Times are not like they were."

I knew that my uncle had felt offended and was angry at me, that he didn't like what I had said and kept quiet only grudgingly. I knew that my father was also angry about what I'd said, believing that I hadn't been directing my words just at my uncle 'Abbas. 'Uthman, the husband of my aunt Hayfa', whose business had flourished and who had acquired a lot of wealth, shook my hand firmly and reckoned that I was embarking on initiatives that would have an influence on the future of the clan.

Leaving aside a few minor irritations, Abu Hanik day was one of the clan's historic days, which although undocumented would be recalled by the clan in their evening gatherings, whenever it occurred to anyone in the clan to recall the deeds and initiatives that I had undertaken.

I had made my peace with Rasmiyya's father a year after our wedding. I knew that he was not at all affected by the pettiness and small-mindedness that poisoned some of the villagers. But when it had all happened, he had feared for his daughter from the more conservative members of his family. He'd expected that he wouldn't be able to protect or defend her, and for this reason he had preferred to keep her in Sheikh

Za'al's house. He was also forced to miss her wedding so as not to be exposed to the others' anger.

When 'Abd al-Fattah came into my house, he embraced Rasmiyya and kissed her on her forehead and both cheeks, and she returned his embrace and kisses. Then her brothers embraced her, and a new page was turned in the relations between us. I didn't know that Rasmiyya's cousin hadn't forgiven me. He hadn't come to my house with the other guests, and I hadn't invited him. I made a banquet for my father-in-law and his sons, wife and daughters, and my father and other family members welcomed them warmly with respect.

Meanwhile, I had discovered that my father-in-law liked telling stories. We listened to him telling of people's suffering in 1948, and about the massacres staged by the Zionist gangs to force them to leave their towns and villages and flee the country.

I found out that he was interested in agriculture, and that he was an expert in pruning trees and grafting different species onto one another. He had a great liking for Ra's al-Naba', and would always come there whenever he had the time, to prune the fruit trees and plant new species unknown to us, as well as grafting shoots from fruit trees onto wild trees that did not yield fruit. As he worked, he would constantly recall his land that he had been expelled from, and the trees there that were dear to his heart.

How happy Rasmiyya had been after her father had come to our house in Ra's al-Naba'. She said she felt a heavy burden had been lifted from her shoulders and that everything had returned to normal.

That night, Rasmiyya and I continued our conversation as we lay in bed, my arm under her head and her hand against my chest. She felt as if that night was the first night of our marriage. She seemed unable to sleep, she was so happy.

We went to sleep a little before dawn, and I stayed asleep until late morning. Rasmiyya stayed sleeping until noon. I was absorbed in studying her radiant face and her hair that was sprawled over the pillow. I didn't want to wake her. She was sound asleep, and I was just happy that she was sleeping deeply, in a way she hadn't done for many nights.

When she opened her eyes, she was surprised to find me looking at her like a humble worshiper. She smiled, and I kissed her cheeks, lips, nose, eyes and hair. She put her arms around my neck.

I was happy when I saw her moving about confidently inside the house and in the courtyard. I kissed her and went about my business, content.

I would meet Sheikh Za'al and we would divide up the money that our men brought back after delivering the goods to the edge of the desert. Several times, I took a risk and helped to guard the goods and deliver them to the requested place. Then my men suggested that I should spare myself the consequences of the risk. I started to follow the action from a certain distance and issue my instructions to the men, after taking in everything they had encountered on their journey and the obstacles they had found in their way. Meanwhile, my men's loyalty to me increased, and they started to call me Sheikh Falihan out of admiration. I liked that as a nickname. I consecrated it by wearing striped abayas over a kumbaz cut from the finest material, with a white or yellow keffiya on my head, and a headband. I acquired a thoroughbred horse, a revolver, a sword and a *rebab*. Sometimes, when necessary, I would wear a suit, with a shirt and tie. After temporarily dispensing with my keffiya and headband, I'd get into my car and take on the appearance of a modern man, with all that that word implies.

But I didn't feel at all at ease. My heart was always pre-occupied with the goods and the men. I was scared the goods would be stolen, despite all the security precautions, and I'd suffer losses and possible bankruptcy. I was afraid that the men—among the best men in the clan—might be murdered. And if any of them was killed, I'd be responsible to his family for his death.

Wadha, my stepmother, started to regard me as an ill omen even more obviously than before. I knew that she didn't like me, and didn't like my mother Mathila, even though the women of the family heaped praise on her. I believe that they were deceived by her. Wadha was like a snake in the grass. She slithered and bit, and was an expert at hiding herself.

6

Wadha

How much I had to put up with from Mathila and her son, Falihan! And how I suffered when we moved from the desert, too. In fact, that suffering hid how much I suffered from Falihan and his mother. Some nights I would be so restless I could only sleep after two hours of tossing and turning in bed. I would shut the front door and lie down beside Mannan. Outside there would be a troubling noise. Mannan would say to me, "That's the sound of the wind." And I would tell him, "That's the sound of our ancestors who were killed in the battles, Mannan. They wake in the night to demand revenge." He'd say to me, "Sleep and trust in God, Wadha." I would reply, "Blessings and goodness are from God," and try to overcome my fear, and to sleep.

In the morning, I would open the windows of the house, asking God to protect me from Satan the accursed and repeating the name of God seven times. I would carry a bucket of water and sprinkle the threshold and the courtyard. Then I would take a bowl of dough and head towards the shelter with the stove and the tin on which I baked the flat bread. I would enter the shelter, right foot first, the name of God on my lips, for I was convinced that this place was haunted.

I lit the fire under the bread tin, and the fire crept through the firewood. I realized that the creatures that dwelled there must be blowing on it to put it out. I fanned it with the edge of my *thob* to make it burn more fiercely. I knew that the fire was a female, but I neither loved nor hated it. I remained in fear of it, though, because it could not be trusted, despite giving us warmth and having other effects that it was impossible to ignore. I was afraid of the creatures that lived here near the fire; I feared the touch of a mad jinni, which could make me lose my mind. Even so, I continued to feed the fire with wood. I pulled off the first lump of dough and molded it with my two hands until it became round as the face of the moon. Then I put it in the tin tray, and carried on doing this until I had used all the dough, keeping my eye on the bread so that it wouldn't get snapped up by the creatures that lived there. I was convinced that they were constantly asking each other about the best way to stop me from coming to their place. But I was forced to come every morning. I'm certain (though God knows best) that they were the cause of my daughter 'Aziza's death.

How beautiful that girl was! She had long hair, and her eyes were wide as cups. She was as tall as her father Mannan. I had her four years after my Muhammad al-Asghar.

When she was ten years old, she complained to me, "My head hurts, Mama!" I lit incense around her and wondered what could have happened to 'Aziza. Maybe it's the evil eye, I thought, or maybe an envious sprite saw her on the way back from school. "Did a woman see you walking along the road, my daughter?" I asked her. She said that she hadn't seen any woman. I was advised that I should sacrifice two sheep for the sake of God most high and fly seven white flags on the roof of the house if 'Aziza recovered. Mahira gave me the name of a fortune-teller who lived in 'Anata, just outside Jerusalem, so I went to the fortune-teller and he wrote a charm for 'Aziza.

Afterwards, I became aware of the mirrors in the house. I realized that Aziza must have looked at the mirror in the bedroom I shared with Mannan. I knew that the mirror was a woman and so could not escape the evil of the jinn. It was after sunset, and 'Aziza had gone into the room to bring me the prayer mat. I went in while she was there, O my God, and she told me she had looked in the mirror. I am certain that the creatures living in the mirror—may God's name be around us everywhere—touched her and hit her on the head. I said, "God help and assist me! Mathila will certainly gloat over my loss, and so will her son Falihan."

■

Muhammad al-Asghar

I remained unable to bridge the rift between my brother Falihan and my mother Wadha. I tried several times without success, but I never stopped trying.

Our days were not all the same. Some days were bitter, but others were full of hope and expectations. When I turned sixteen, my mother looked at me admiringly, praising me for my height, which I had inherited from my father. "You're the camel of the family, and its best protector," she said. I was convinced that this was too much to say about a youth at the beginning of his life. But my mother, it seems, had her excuses for saying something that might have been a little premature and for publicizing it so freely.

It was the time of the 1956 national elections. There were fierce political discussions in homes, clubs, cafés and everywhere else. My brother Falihan thought of putting himself forward for parliament but heeded my father's advice to abandon the idea because of the intense competition, which made the chances of his success extremely unlikely.

My father joined the National Socialist Party. He said that he'd met the leader of the party in Amman and admired the serious and measured way that he had spoken. He said that he was a friend of the party's candidate in Jerusalem, who was a well-known lawyer, and that he had previously fulfilled a number of my father's requests when he had visited him in his office.

My father assembled the men of the clan in his guest room and urged them to cast their votes for his lawyer friend. He was surprised to discover that the al-'Abd al-Lat clan, which used to accept his advice, was no longer the same clan. Some men said that they were with the Ba'thists and were promoting their slogan, which they waved in the face of the communists—"No East and no West." Others said that they were with the Communist Party candidate contesting the Christian seat, a Jordanian doctor who came from Karak to treat patients in Jerusalem. My brother Muhammad al-Kabir said, "I am with the doctor, because he is the candidate of the poor, and he's against injustice and exploitation." His supporters began repeating the slogan that they had often used in demonstrations: "Our demands are those of the people—bread, peace, and freedom." They often reminded us of the victory that the Soviet Union had achieved over the Nazis.

One of my cousins said that he supported Hizb al-Tahrir. He said that wicked people did not respect the opposite viewpoint. They had wronged this pious sheikh by defacing his electoral propaganda written in red ink on walls, and mutilating his name so that it could no longer be read correctly. He said, "The only solution to the problems of this nation is the restoration of the Islamic caliphate."

My brother Falihan said, "I'm with the villagers' candidate. Like me, he supports the monarchy and he's a person that fought in defense of Palestine." My other brother, Muhammad al-Saghir, said, "These elections are a Western innovation. We should seek guidance from a formal religious council." Then he cited some verses from the Qur'an.

My father didn't feel comfortable when he saw the clan going in different directions. He was sure that it had become more disunited. My brother Muhammad al-Kabir made clear in his presence that the time of tribal allegiances was past and that now was the time of allegiance to the homeland.

My father coughed and was about to launch into an extended song in praise of the clan and an enumeration of its glories, but kept silent as he saw the clansmen clapping to signify their approval of what my brother, Muhammad al-Kabir, had said. He wrapped himself in his kefiyya so that it covered his whole face, apart from his eyes, which lit up with anger. No one paid any attention to his anger, however, and my brother, Muhammad al-Kabir, said, "We must respect pluralism."

As the clansmen clapped, my father scrutinized their faces, astonishment written on his own face at this new phenomenon—applause—which his guest room had never witnessed before. When the clansmen had wanted to express their support for him, they had usually waved their hands, clutching their swords or rifles, and said, "For your eyes, Sheikh Mannan, rejoice, we are with you!"

My father tried not to escalate the situation. When he saw the world changing around him, he found that it was better for him to swim with the tide, so as not to lose the respect of the clan. If his son, the fruit of his loins, took an opposite view, he had to accept reality, even if it was only on the surface. He removed the covering from his face and remained silent for a few moments, then spoke, as if to offer a comment on what my brother, Muhammad al-Kabir, had said about pluralism: "Okay, let everyone sing the song that is in his head!"

The young clansmen clapped for my father in a way he hadn't expected. His features lit up, then he looked towards me and asked me, intending it as a joke, "Come on, Muhammad al-Asghar, who will you give your vote to?"

I smiled and didn't reply, for I didn't have a vote yet. But his question spurred me to look for a reply. "You asked me, and I must try to find an answer," I told him later.

"Muhammad, my son," my mother said, "you're the camel of the family." Then she hummed a song that I'd often heard in tribal gatherings.

> Tonight again, my loved ones,
> the family camel's come home!

I thanked her for her confidence in me and said, "I shall look carefully for an answer and hope not to lose my way as my brother Falihan did."

When Falihan learned what I'd said about him, he said to me, "You don't know anything about life yet. I haven't lost my way, for life has many paths, and I have chosen the way that suits me."

"That's your brother Falihan," my mother said, "a bad knot. Take care to keep away from him."

When my brother Falihan found out what my mother had said about him, he told me off and said, "Your mother, Wadha, uses wrongful language against me."

"Falihan, my brother," I replied, trying to ease the tension between them, "my mother has only good in her heart towards you."

"Your mother harbors evil towards me, just as she does towards our brother Muhammad al-Kabir."

After the elections, my brother Muhammad al-Kabir became the target of criticism of a new kind. The palace dissolved the national government, political parties were suspended, and those belonging to them were interned. An exception was made for the Muslim Brotherhood, which maintained that it was a missionary organization whose work was the reform of the individual with the aim of reforming society, so the regime embraced it.

My brother Muhammad al-Kabir was interned, and the whole country was subjected to large-scale search operations conducted by the army and security services. My mother was afraid, and I didn't take part in any political activities. I took part in a demonstration against the Baghdad Pact before going off to my lessons, but I took no interest in politics despite the attempts of my brother Muhammad al-Kabir and his wife Maryam to influence me. Every evening my mother would light incense for me.

One morning, army personnel were deployed in Ra's al-Naba' and raided several houses. They searched cupboards and drawers, they searched the kitchens and felt the sacks of wheat and barley, looking for weapons and for Communist books and pamphlets. They searched my schoolbooks without finding anything that could constitute a danger to the state. Meanwhile, my mother never stopped reciting charms to ward off evil.

As the atmosphere in the country grew more repressive, my father abandoned politics and contented himself with following the news broadcasts.

My mother's fears increased, not just of the repressive policies but also of the people who were living in the same place as us, listening to our conversations and watching both where we moved and where we stopped. She said that she no longer went out at night to check our animals in the pen because one night she had seen a spy running along the streets. She had followed his movements by the light that shone from him. Then he disappeared down the well by the foot of the mountain. She said that after that she avoided going out at night.

When she was forced to fetch water from the well after sunset, she no longer opened the door to the well without first mentioning the name of God seven times. As she let down the bucket deep into the well, then pulled it up again, she continued to repeat the name of God to ward off the jinn and stop them from clinging to the bucket.

The women of the family accused my mother Wadha of putting fear into their hearts. She could find no one to support her except for my father's uncle, 'Abd al-Jabbar, who claimed that the jinn visited him at night and grabbed his hands and feet, lifting him up and flinging his body in the air before returning it to the bed to carry on sleeping beside Mahira in safety.

But the jinn's doings didn't stop there. Sometimes, Mahira would wake up and not find 'Abd al-Jabbar beside her in bed. (Mahira was now an old lady who no longer moved across the tiles like a dove. She limped a little whenever she walked because of a pain in her legs.) She knew that he had crept into the bed of her co-wife Khadija, but when Mahira confronted him with it, he would tell her—swearing the most solemn of oaths—that it was the jinn who had carried him off while he slept and thrown him in Khadija's bed, then left the house without offering any explanation for their behavior. And anyway, how could he ask them for an explanation while he was asleep? And besides, why should they bother to present 'Abd al-Jabbar with any explanations?

My mother used his explanations as support for her attitudes, despite the implicit threat to her friendship that linked her with Mahira. She undertook several preventative measures so that the jinn would not attack her. She covered the mirrors with thin cloth, believing that looking at them at night would make someone mad or possessed. She only realized this one night when she noticed a shadow in the gloom moving inside the mirror and was stricken with terror. She wondered how she had failed to notice the danger lurking inside the mirrors when my father had bought her her first mirror years ago. She had celebrated and embraced it at the time, and she looked at her face in it night and day.

She wasn't content to assert that the jinn lived with us. She was convinced that the place where my father built our house was inhabited by the souls of our ancestors who had fought and been killed, and their blood flowed over the earth. Their ghosts would set out at night looking for an opportunity for revenge, or to remind us of what used to be. My mother would hear the clink of swords and the neighing of horses in the night, with cries for help and the sounds of sighing and groaning. The result would be that my mother became so restless she could not sleep.

She wouldn't sleep until the threshold of the house had been sprinkled with water. Meanwhile, she would repeat the name of God and recite charms and verses from the Qur'an, to temper the rashness of the jinn who dwelled with us, as well as the eagerness of the ancestors to lap up the water that quenched their thirst and reduced their appetite for seeking revenge.

She revealed her fears to me and told me a part of them, warning me not to sprinkle water on the threshold without invoking the name of God, because it might fall on the head of a jinni, who would be angry at me, take possession of me, and make me lose my mind. When the family went to bed and I was alone in the quiet of the night, engrossed in my lessons, I would be overcome by fear, and imagine the jinn standing behind the window, watching me, finding it strange that I was still awake. They naturally weren't interested in the fact that any diligent student was forced to stay up late, and this made them even more inclined to expose me to all sorts of suffering. I imagined the ancestors standing behind the window in the same way, as if they were in league with the jinn, stroking their beards as they gazed at me, reckoning among themselves that I wouldn't be seeking vengeance on them and would forget about them as I continued to immerse myself in my books, which didn't concern them in the least.

I became more and more agitated, and wondered if I should I keep studying or go to bed. I avoided looking at the window, afraid of an unpleasant surprise. Instead, I went to bed, figuring I could spend enough time on my lessons during the day, then go to bed early in the evening, without provoking either the jinn or the spirits of the ancestors. My mother was relieved.

7

Muhammad al-Asghar

When electricity arrived in Ra's al-Naba' in 1965, my mother Wadha received a shock she hadn't anticipated, or even thought about before. Darkness always aroused a lot of fear in her. She was convinced that darkness was an evil woman, dedicated to embracing the jinn. But now it seemed to her that her fear of the jinn would not continue in the same way, forever. This realization came when she saw some workmen wearing protective helmets, looking like soldiers preparing for war. Perched on ladders, they were running rubber-coated wires into houses. Then they'd install control switches on the walls, so that every nook and cranny of the house interior could be illuminated.

Visible changes occurred in my mother's life, and in all our lives. I was twenty-five. These changes reached us five years before they reached our neighbors in the village of al-Sawahira al-Gharbiyya. Houses acquired refrigerators, washing machines, cookers, vacuum cleaners, televisions. My mother avoided watching television and didn't follow the programs like the other women of the family, as she believed that TV, like the radio, was inhabited by jinn—males, who appeared on the screen with trimmed mustaches and neat ties, and females, who had no hesitation about shamelessly exposing parts of their bodies.

Over time, my mother's stories lost some of their previous appeal. She would look for an evening gathering, but find one only with some difficulty. The family had begun to exchange her live storytelling for television soaps, dramas adapted for the screen, concerts by popular singers—broadcast live or recorded. This did not harbinger well for my mother, who regarded all this as an interference with the details of her life and an affront to her lifestyle.

Even so, her eagerness to tell stories never waned, although she did change her style. My mother realized that she had to stop repeating herself, telling the same story time after time. She began to pay more attention to her audience's mood, pausing at key moments, summarizing her meaning in a few words, and finishing when she saw someone in the audience fidgeting or not wanting to listen. She also stopped telling stories that everyone already knew, instead relating (though not at great length) news of the clan that she picked up from other women when they met at a morning or evening gathering. She would then filter what she'd heard and retell it in a way that appealed to her, often refreshed with caustic comments and snide remarks that she added spontaneously.

She continued to avoid watching television programs or using washing machines. She said washing machines were inhabited by jinn, that it was the jinn's hands that agitated the clothes moving around inside them. She continued to wash her clothes, and her husband's, by hand, saying this would assure that their bodies would stay healthy.

She tried to live her life free from the influences and conveniences of civilization that had arrived in Ra's al-Naba', though she grumbled whenever the electricity was interrupted and the house plunged into darkness. Once again, she would tell everyone that darkness was her mortal enemy. She would cautiously search for the kerosene lamp, or "Lux," as it was called, to light up this or that, while she waited for the electricity to come back on. When it did come back, she would heave a sigh of relief and praise God, more convinced than ever that electricity was simply the light of the angels sent by God (May He be exalted!) to light up the land, as a kindness to His servants.

Then she gradually spoke less about the jinn, perhaps because the electricity had conquered the darkness, except when it was cut off for some reason. Almost all her fears sprang from darkness, and the dangers, surprises and secrets that it contained, as well as the jinn and devils that lurked there.

Despite that, her attitude about television remained largely unchanged, although she no longer repeated her previous convictions that the people who appeared on the screen—male and female alike—were jinn. When she threw a passing glance at the screen and saw women dancing and exposing their legs to everyone, she merely said they were whores, then went off to her room to say her prayers.

The refrigerator, however, she couldn't boycott for very long. She could see how much time it saved her when she didn't have to cook every day! She could cook enough food for two days, so she'd get a break from cooking for one day. She praised her Lord for this blessing, but she couldn't get out of her head the fact that the jinn kept watching for her in all sorts of places, especially when they were hatching their evil schemes to cut off the electricity and enjoy the darkness they so loved, and which gave them cover to do as they pleased.

From time to time, I tried to calm her fears, but she could not believe that I had rid myself of my own fears and become someone who could give her advice.

■

My job in the sharia court gave me opportunities to attend the sessions held in the judge's office to examine divorce cases. I recorded the minutes, which often made me perspire. From the start, I was aware of the sensitive nature of my role, despite the fact that it was an ordinary low-grade employee's position, for I had a certain amount of access to some of the inner workings of families in the city and surrounding villages.

After getting home, I would record in my own personal notebook the cases I'd become acquainted with, and which in a way had become part of my life. Sometimes, especially after reading Yusuf Idris's novel *al-Haram*, I anticipated that someday I'd be able to successfully write about social issues of concern to people. To achieve that, I would make the cases I was recording in my notebook my writing instructor. I imagined people following my articles as serialized episodes in the daily press, and I would feel content.

I dreamt a lot and started to practice writing by recording events, and by replying to the letters that my brother 'Atwan sent from Brazil, as well as those that my brother Salman sent from Kuwait. I'd read their letters to my father, then prepare myself to reply to them in language that I tried hard to make formal and free from errors.

One evening, my father said to me, "What have you done to the family, Muhammad?" Distressed and troubled, he didn't wait for an answer. "Our family is becoming more and more divided," he continued, "just like the al-'Abd al-Lat clan that we belong to." My mother supported him, regarding it as a sign of God's displeasure. She burned a lot of incense throughout our house, as well as sprinkling water over the threshold, covering the mirrors with a light cloth and reciting charms. She became keen to tear off small pieces of clothing from women she didn't like, without their noticing, so that she could burn them at the proper time to protect her children (male and female alike) from their envy and ward off their evil from the family.

My father didn't agree that he was suffering from God's anger. He was confident that God (may His power be exalted!) would not concern himself with devising small misfortunes that were of no value in the scale of His wisdom and might. He became convinced of this when my brother 'Atwan, the younger brother of Falihan, and a son of Mathila, traveled to Brazil to work as a peddler. Reports of the wealth to be made in Brazil, and the job opportunities to be found there, spread through the clan, through Ra's al-Naba', and all over the land, so that people with passports started wanting them to include the ridiculous expression "All countries and Brazil," in the list of countries for which they were valid—as if Brazil was not itself a country!

My brother 'Atwan arrived in Rio de Janeiro with three other clansmen. Several letters arrived from him, describing his life in Brazil, as well as relating news of himself and other members of the clan there.

Rio de Janeiro
December 19, 1958

A fair greeting, gentler than a breeze, at morning and evening, from a wounded heart to my father Mannan, my heart's beloved, hoping of God, the merciful and forgiving, that this letter will find you well, in good heart and in the best of health. If you should wonder about me, I am well, thanks to God, and my health is excellent. I lack nothing except to see you, to talk with you, and to reassure myself about you.

I arrived in Brazil, Father, on December 9. The airplane landed at Rio de Janeiro airport at night. I was with three other members of our clan. I was so sad to be leaving you when we said goodbye at Qalandia airport! God knows when we will meet again after this journey, I said to myself. I won't hide from you the fact that I was happy to be boarding an airplane for the first time in my life and traveling to look for work. We had a three-hour stop in the airport in Paris, where I observed all sorts of men and women wandering through the terminals, or hurrying to catch their flights. When I saw an immodest woman, I looked away, though to be honest, my colleagues behaved in exactly the opposite way. Your understanding is sufficient, father.

After a wait, they called passengers traveling to Rio de Janeiro on loudspeakers in the terminal buildings. We headed for the airplane, and for the second time I became frightened, when the airline hostess started to explain to us what we should do in the event of an emergency while we were in the air. My stomach turned again when the plane took off. Then, as the hostesses walked along the aisle offering refreshments to the passengers, I began to relax. I asked for an orange juice and began to enjoy the view through the window of the masses of clouds floating in the sky. I ate my meal sitting in my seat, with a foreign woman sitting beside me, absorbed in browsing through an illustrated magazine.

I slept for two or three hours. When we were about due to land and the captain asked us to fasten our seatbelts, I felt afraid again. Then I looked at the lights of the city, which stretched into the distance. The aircraft touched down, and after a short wait we disembarked. The weather was neither too hot nor too cold, quite unlike the cold winter weather at this time of the year in our country.

Forgive me for going on so long, Father. We spent three nights in a hotel before finding a house in a modest neighborhood in the city suburbs. The rent isn't too bad, and I'm sharing it with my fellow clansmen.

We go out in the morning and don't return until evening. We travel to the outlying suburbs and go around to the houses, selling women clothes for themselves and their children, and charms and perfumes. We split up and disperse through the various suburbs and don't meet up again until we return home.

My fellow clansmen here send you a thousand greetings and kiss your hand, and I too send you a thousand greetings and kiss your hand. I send from here a thousand greetings for my mother Mathila, and to my brothers and sisters, in particular, Muhammad al-Kabir, Muhammad al-Saghir, Falihan, Falha, Salman (did he send you a letter from Kuwait?), Adham (is there any news of him in Holland?), and Muhammad al-Asghar, may God protect them! A thousand greetings from me to the members of the al-'Abd al-Lat clan, and a thousand greetings to my wife Fahima and my son Mannan, and the same to anyone who asks about me in your part of the world. Farewell and greetings until we meet again in another letter.

P.S. Please reassure me about the news of my brother Muhammad al-Kabir in prison. Hoping for him a speedy release. Please send me the address of my brother Salman and my cousins who traveled to Kuwait, so that I may correspond with them and reassure myself about them. God grant us and them success. Amen, Lord of the Worlds!

Your loving son,
'Atwan Mannan al-'Abd al-Lat

Over time, I was eager to follow the news of my brother 'Atwan in Brazil, as well as news of my brother Salman in Kuwait.

■

I was convinced that my first day on the job at the sharia court would be happy and unforgettable. I put on my new suit and boarded the bus, which took me from Ra's al-Naba' to Jerusalem. I got off near Herod's Gate and walked along the sidewalk of Salah al-Din Street. The stores were open, and men and women were walking along the sidewalk, some quickly and others strolling. Car horns blared in the street for no apparent reason. I saw the city opening like a rose in the morning and felt optimistic and full of life.

I climbed the steps to the building and entered the sharia court. I greeted my fellow employees and introduced myself to them. They welcomed me, and the head of section responsible for me in the post took me around the court departments. There were two women whom I greeted without a handshake in response to their wishes. Then he took me into the boss's office. I greeted him, and after a number of questions he wished me success in my job.

In a large, rectangular room, where three employees were stationed, I found a wooden chair waiting for me, facing a table with fading paint. On it were files and registers with cardboard covers. I opened the register that I would open constantly for years, sitting on this chair, at this table.

But I will never forget my first day on the job, as it was the gate through which I passed on my way to the struggle of life.

■

In another letter from 'Atwan we learned that on one occasion, a heavily built man had attacked and beaten him unmercifully. His fellow clansmen saw what was happening to him but didn't dare come to his aid, or even intervene to stop the attack on him.

Rio de Janeiro
June 3, 1959

The fact is, Father, that despite the difficulties that face me here, you are always in my mind, and you have accustomed me to truth and honesty. You know how much I love my wife Fahima, and how much I love my son Mannan! It is pride enough for me that Mannan bears your name. May God grant you health, and keep you as a crown on our heads.

It is also true that being away from home like this weighs on me like a mountain, and if a man can't bear it he will collapse. I won't disappoint your expectations of me, because you are the father of men. I will tell you that some weeks ago I left the house where I was staying with my fellow clansmen. They all have tempers, Father, and sometimes there were misunderstandings between us for the most trivial reasons. Abroad, everyone becomes incapable of putting up with the people who are closest to them if their tempers are not right. What really hurt me was that I was exposed to aggression from someone in this country. I sold him some pants, and when he washed them they shrank. He came to me angry. I'd sold him the pants sitting on the sidewalk in front of the house where we were staying, with a case of goods in front of me, and my three fellow clansmen nearby displaying their wares as well. He recognized me and started beating me, and I couldn't resist him because of his size. I expected my friends to help me, but they were too afraid.

If they had at least intervened, they might have stopped him. He kept on until I collapsed on the ground, and unfortunately there were no police in the vicinity, and no passersby intervened. I was in pain for the whole night, racked by regret that I had come here and thinking of going back to where I had come from, for in my country I could live safely among my own family.

The important thing, Father, is that my colleagues showed that they were sorry. They said a lot of things to excuse their inaction. But in the moments when they were honest with themselves, they blamed themselves and encouraged me to submit a complaint to the police. I feared the consequences of any complaint. The assailant might deny everything, and they might not be able to arrest him, because I didn't know his name or where he lived. So I tore up this page and remain hurt and wounded whenever I recall it.

I have rented a house near to the house where my fellow clansmen are staying. I shall live on my own like this until God grants me a way out. I hope you will forgive me, Father, because I have not sent you any money even though I have been here for six months. When we change the money into dollars, it loses a lot of its value. I hope you will be patient with me, and look after my wife and child until I am able to send you money.

P.S. I received a letter from my brother Salman. He said that he was working in a gas station and is living in a house with five clansmen, but the thing that annoys him most is the hot weather in Kuwait.

I send a thousand greetings from abroad to anyone who asks about me. Farewell, and greetings.

Your loving son,
'Atwan

When this news from 'Atwan reached us, my father was angry. He said he wished he had been there to support his wronged son, then heaped curses on the clansmen, whose blood hadn't stirred in their veins as they watched 'Atwan being beaten. "Shame on you, my clansmen!" he shouted in a wounded voice.

Of course, the clansmen had been afraid of the possible consequences of intervening against the Brazilian, who might seek help from his friends, and the affair might have developed to an extent that the police intervened and the clansmen were put in prison—which might have led to their being deported.

On the other hand, my brother Falihan dismissed 'Atwan, saying that he "prattles a lot" and that when he traveled to Brazil, 'Atwan imagined that he would find gold piled up in the streets and that he would only have to fill his pockets and bring it back home. Falihan said that 'Atwan didn't concern him one bit, and nor did the family. That he preferred to leave family affairs to me and occupy himself with his own business, which takes up all his time. He has his own life and memories.

Falihan

When Salwa sang her famous song "Where? To Ramallah!" I fell in love with it. I took Rasmiyya in my Cadillac to the restaurant in the Harb Hotel in Ramallah. I thought about how she and I would have dinner and eat the choicest food, and afterwards I would smoke a *narghileh* and relax.

We arrived there at sunset. The city was alive with a free-and-easy atmosphere, despite being full of people who had been forced to flee in 1948. People were strolling along al-Irsal

Street—men in smart suits, youths in beach shorts, and girls in short skirts that showed their thighs and colored blouses that showed their arms. I could see secret policemen scattered among the crowds, whose job was to watch members of forbidden parties. I wasn't afraid of them because I supported the regime.

We went into the restaurant and ordered a dinner of grilled meat, with salads and pickles. I asked the waiter to play us the song sung by Salwa. We listened to it and it made our evening seem like jasmine. Then we listened to songs by Farid al-Atrash, 'Abd al-Halim Hafez, and Sabah. When Sabah sang "To 'Usfuriyya, to 'Usfuriyya," Rasmiyya and I were very happy. At a nearby table there were three men and three women eating supper and drinking wine. A tall, seductive woman stood up, tied a handkerchief around her waist and danced.

Rasmiyya looked shyly at the woman who was dancing, her body swaying like a willow branch, and at the men who were shaking their hips as they sat on their chairs, their eyes fixed on the woman's body. I loved Rasmiyya's combination of shyness with a desire that could easily be seen.

We went back to the house. Rasmiyya went into the bathroom and washed her body, and I took a shower. She appeared in the bedroom wearing her nightdress, which didn't cover her knees. I put on a record with the song "Where? To Ramallah" on it, and she stood combing and plaiting her hair in front of the mirror, as she gently shook her hips and swayed to the rhythm of the song. I lay on the bed watching her body, thanking the Creator who had given her such beauty.

When the summer festivals became popular in Ramallah, I was the first to support them. I loved these festivals, which made people from Kuwait and the other countries of the Gulf come to visit Ramallah for their summer vacation, to enjoy its moderate climate and healthy atmosphere. They would rent houses to stay in for the summer, or sleep in hotels. They would stroll along the sidewalks in the balmy evenings with their wives and daughters, the men in white dishdashas, the women in black silk abayas, with multicolored dresses hidden beneath them and silk kerchiefs over their heads. All sorts of people would come from Jerusalem, Amman and other places, wanting to spend a pleasant time, and Ramallah would seem proud of its visitors. The air would resound with songs sung by both male and female entertainers. I would hanker after the songs of Samira Tawfiq and wish that she could come to one of the festivals so that I could watch her and enjoy her singing with a passion that would never end.

I was filled with happiness when I saw that Rasmiyya also enjoyed the summer evenings, and I promised her that we would go to visit Ramallah often. We would sit in the parks and watch musical theater performances that told the story of Ramallah, and of its sons who had emigrated to the mahjar, the diaspora, in search of a livelihood, then settled in the USA and countries in South America. Many of them, in fact, came back in the summer, so that the summer nights in Ramallah were even more full of song and happiness.

We returned to Ra's al-Naba' late at night. Rasmiyya slipped lightly into the house from the car so as not to be spotted by any of the men or women of the family, but she did not always succeed in escaping notice.

The following day, the women of the family would some-times just nod and wink at her, while at other times they would criticize her openly. "How can you leave your children on their own and stay out for half the night? How can you agree to put on high-heeled shoes and stagger around all over the place like a dove with a broken wing, always in danger of falling over and exposing every part of your body?"

"My friends, I haven't done anything wrong!" she would reply. She would invent all sorts of excuses, but to no avail. I would plead with her not to take any notice of them, and tell her that it was jealousy that was leading them to make insinuations about her and try to put her down. She would be persuaded by my words and resolve to take no notice, but would quickly become nervous again. "I can't stand the things they say," she told me. She was convinced that they gossiped behind her back when she wasn't sitting with them.

When they began to get even more involved in the details of her life, we adopted a different approach, to spare her any suffering. We would go to Ramallah to spend the evening there, then return at midnight to our other house, which was situated near the al-'Awda camp, on the road between Ramallah and Jerusalem. In this way, our comings and goings were not as visible as they were in Ra's al-Naba'. I did that to protect her frame of mind, for she couldn't bear any of the women of the family (or anyone else, for that matter) to interfere with her dealings or lifestyle.

I never stopped being uneasy, though. My father Mannan often said to me, "Dirty money does not last." I somehow realized that what he was saying was right and that his words were directed at me rather than anyone else. I have a lot of money, I thought, and before I waste it on parties and gatherings, feasts and excursions, extravagant cars, new houses with posh furniture, and the best clothes, I should invest it in things that will be useful to me in my old age and the coming years, when I do not know what the fates will hold in store for me. For God alone knows these things.

I bought five stores in a number of markets in Jerusalem. I turned one of them into a café and another into a restaurant. A third sold electrical goods; the fourth sold clothes and materials for women and children, and the fifth was an exchange office. I relied on a number of clansmen to work in them for monthly salaries that I found acceptable but the others found too low, so that I was accused of meanness and of exploiting the people closest to me. My brother 'Atwan worked in the clothing store for a whole year, then said that he was barely making enough money to support his wife and son. So he left his job in the store and traveled to Brazil.

I bought a mountain near the camp where my wife's family and my sister Falha lived. I set up a quarry on my mountain, to hew rocks and shape them so that they were suitable for house building. My brother-in-law worked in the quarry, because his job as an itinerant sweet seller no longer provided him and his wife and children with enough money. My father-in-law also worked there, because his job pruning trees at certain times of the year no longer provided him with sufficient income.

With time, my business expanded to take account of people's need for radio and television sets, as well as refrigerators, washing machines and vacuum cleaners. I started to sell them on lease, and also started granting some customers easy loans on the basis that they would pay them back in installments with interest at fixed times. My father, may God forgive him, called this usury, forbidden by God, but I called it legitimate trade as practiced by the banks and every other trading organization in the world.

I took no notice of what was being said (which reached me by various channels) to the effect that I was exploiting the residents of the camp, including my father-in-law and his relations, as well as my brother-in-law and his relations, in order to amass enormous wealth. Meanwhile, they remained as poor as before as a result of having to flee their towns and villages, and being forced to remain in a wretched camp while they waited to return to their original homes. I put up with all this talk for Rasmiyya and Falha's sake, and I put up with it because I regarded it as untrue.

The whole time, I was concerned about Rasmiyya. She hesitated when I suggested to her that she should take off her embroidered *thob* and wear a maxi dress. I said to her, "You and I go together to the parks and restaurants in Ramallah, and a maxi dress will be better for the evenings." After some coyness and procrastination, she looked younger than she was when she put it on. It wasn't anything new, as the maxi fashion had already spread and made its way from the city to the villages. I said to her, "The maxi dress covers the whole body, and it's modest and attractive at the same time." I bought her a number of different colored dresses and gave them to her as a present on our wedding anniversary. She usually went with the women of the family to Jerusalem to buy dresses, skirts, underwear, perfumes and makeup.

The fashion for short skirts also spread through the town. They were worn by teenagers, and by some office and bank employees, and women who worked in companies and institutions. The skirts exposed a woman's thighs in an eye-catching fashion, which made the men of our clan forbid their teenage daughters to wear them. My brother Muhammad al-Saghir devoted a sermon to them in the Ra's al-Naba' mosque, in which he said that any woman who wore this lewd sort of garment would come to the Day of Resurrection naked and would be hurled into the fire. His sermon left such an impression on people that looking at a skirt became tainted with feelings of revulsion.

During this period, the fashion for japonaise blouses also gained ground, which left a woman's arms exposed. As a result, girls in the city started to avoid vaccinations against infectious diseases in the upper arm, because they left a permanent mark on the skin, and instead had the injections at the top of their thigh. But no woman in Ra's al-Naba' dared to wear a japonaise skirt or blouse.

Rasmiyya didn't think of wearing them because she thought that they were only suitable for women in their twenties, and she herself was now in her thirties. She was also sensitive about anything connected with her behavior, and never forgot that her co-wife Sheikha would insult her whenever she clashed or quarreled with her by saying that she had married me in the absence of her father. Then, when the quarrel got worse, she would accuse her of having acted dishonorably by showing me her body on the grass on the open ground before we were married. I don't know how this talk had found its way to Sheikha despite my efforts to keep it restricted to the tightest circle possible.

I didn't try to encourage her to wear a japonaise skirt or blouse. I bought her a skirt and blouse to wear at home when we were alone, and I enjoyed seeing how the beauty of her body took shape, half hidden and half revealed.

Rasmiyya was not content to wear them at home. She started to go out into the courtyard of the house and walk about under the spring sun wearing them. Then she started to go out to hang the wash on the line in the courtyard, where she could be seen by her co-wife Sheikha and some of the women of the family. Rumors about her began to fly. The women accused her of being a badly brought-up slut, who left her house half-naked to tempt the devils, so that she could enjoy them looking at her body, and indeed doing more than look.

When their loathing for her reached its peak, they stopped uttering her name, and referred to her just as the *fallaha*. She didn't mind that, as she was in fact a peasant. Sheikha and the other women's conceit reached such a point that they resorted to making fun of her by calling her a refugee. She was indeed a refugee. But the fate that had befallen her and her family, as well as hundreds of thousands of other Palestinian men and women, was not of her or their doing. And Sheikha and the women of the family should have been ashamed of themselves in using this description to abuse her or show her in a bad light.

I said this to Sheikha when her words got back to me, and I asked her and the other women of the family not to repeat them again. I tried to placate Rasmiyya by kissing her head and forehead and cheeks. I tried to persuade her that this women's talk was just an expression of their jealousy of her, or it would not have crossed their minds and they wouldn't have said it. After that, she returned to being her usual generous self.

I had encouraged her to wear dresses that covered the knee but left the rest of her legs uncovered. She hesitated, then went along with my wishes after noticing how this fashion was spreading in the city, even though it wasn't yet very common in Ra's al-Naba'—though some educated women in the village had started to wear dresses in imitation of the women in the city. After a slight hesitation, these dresses began to be worn by some girls in our family who had been to school and graduated. They told any mother or father who objected to what they were doing that they were imitating Nawal, the daughter of Najma and 'Abd al-Wadud, who lived in the city and wore dresses every day.

■

Rio de Janeiro
December 3, 1961

I can tell you, Father, that I am very industrious in earning a living. I get up early in the morning, rinse my face with a little water, have breakfast, then pick up my bag of goods, put my trust in God and travel to the outlying suburbs. There I stop in front of people's doors and shout loudly, hoping the residents will buy my goods. The women come out with their children, who try to play with the goods as I display them in front of their mothers. I shoo them away, and the mothers do the same, absorbed in examining the clothes and turning them over in their hands. They buy colored dresses for themselves, as well as skirts and underwear, while for their children they buy pants, shirts and socks. They pay for their purchases and I thank them, and go on from one house to the next.

Some houses don't open their doors. In some of them, women who aren't prepared to buy clothes from a traveling salesman look out from the windows, making gestures with their hands to show that they don't want to buy anything. I put up with the situation and don't get angry because this is to be expected. It's not reasonable that every woman should come out to buy. It's true that I'm embarking on a new experiment, Father, getting to know all sorts of new people and finding pleasure in earning an honest living. But some nights I feel uneasy and unable to sleep, when I recall sitting in your guest room, chatting and laughing, and recalling how Palestine used to be and what it has become! We ask for mercy on the souls of the martyrs, and ask God's mercy on the Palestinians who were honored and exalted in their towns and villages, then became refugees.

I remember the advice of my mother, Mathila, to me, to hide my white money for a black day. I am putting that advice into practice and only spending enough to cover my food and clothing requirements. The rest I am saving to send to you and my wife and child. I tell you frankly, Father, I cannot sleep when I think about Fahima and Mannan. But this doesn't happen to me every night. Quite often I sleep like a log, because I come back from my rounds feeling tired, put my head on the pillow and sleep until morning.

And because I miss you and Mother, I hope that you will honor me by going to Jerusalem, to Hagopian the photographer, to take a picture of you and Mother and send it to me so that I can keep it and kiss it every morning. And because I miss Fahima and Mannan (your understanding is enough, Father), I ask you to take them to the photographer too and send their picture so that I may look at them constantly. From here I send a thousand greetings to all who inquire about me. Farewell, and greetings.

Your loving son,
'Atwan Mannan

8

Muhammad al-Asghar

I was keen on watching films. I loved Maryam Fakhr al-Din's acting, as well as Fatin Hamama and Magda. I loved Shadiya, Faiza Ahmad, Sabah, and Hoda Sultan's singing. Before I was employed at the sharia court, I wanted to become an actor. I thought I would go to university in Cairo, where I'd meet a cinema producer and ask him to give me a part in one of his films.

I must have had a vivid imagination. How could I get to know a cinema producer when I was just an unknown student? And how could he be persuaded to give me a part in one of his films unless I decided to study acting in the Academy of Arts? That might be different, but I wasn't interested in studying acting. I believed it was possible to practice it as a hobby, like the careers of a number of Egyptian actors.

When I began working at the sharia court, my desire to act evaporated. The reasons were the place where I was working and my father's financial circumstances, which had deteriorated year after year. He thought that if I held a job, he could be relieved of arranging the finances required for university study. I understood his view and was happy to accept the position.

When I started recording in my notebook the revelations of women who wanted to divorce their husbands, and men who wanted to divorce their wives, I believed that with the details, stories and facts that I was accumulating, I would in time be able to write chapters of a long novel that would shake the foundations of our patriarchal society—a society that repressed and wronged women, and denied them their rights and dignity. I saw a connection between wronging women and losing the country, and told some friends that we would not be able to free the country as long as women were oppressed.

I tried several times to write some lines of a story, without coming up with anything I was satisfied with. I almost ripped up my notebook. I was thinking that later on I might be able to write a film script showing the injustices women suffered. This idea came to mind after I'd seen a number of films starring Maryam Fakhr al-Din in different roles, especially ones about the oppressed situation of women.

I vowed I would write a film script using the material I had. I became engrossed in observing people's behavior, especially the younger members of the family. The task that my father had entrusted me compelled me to do just that.

My father was constantly complaining about the state of our country. Informers prowled the streets without even disguising what they were doing, which made people scared. Perhaps they appeared undisguised in public places deliberately, in order to strike added fear into people's minds. My mother Wadha was becoming more frightened, taking every opportunity to ask God's protection from the wickedness of Satan. "I'm afraid for you, Muhammad, my son," she would say to me, "and for the girls and boys."

My brother Muhammad al-Kabir had been in prison for five years. His wife, Maryam, regularly visited him there. My father visited him occasionally and came back from his visits sad and worried about him, wasting his life away in prison. The lawyer told him that his son would be released if he renounced the Communist Party and published his renunciation in the daily paper. My father became enthusiastic and said that that was easy.

My brother Falihan said, "If I were in the position of my brother Muhammad the Elder, I would renounce the party ten times, not just once, announce my allegiance to His Highness the King and the regime, and sign my name clearly and un-equivocally under the renunciation."

My father went to my brother and demanded that he sign the renunciation formula that the lawyer had drawn up. Clearly puzzled, he told me that my brother had seized the piece of paper and torn it up, saying that he would not renounce the party even if he remained in jail for a hundred years.

My mother said, "Your father, Muhammad, my son, came back furious and said to me, 'Would it be the end of the world if he had just put his signature on the piece of paper and come out of prison!'

"I told Mannan to trust in God," she said, "and not be angry. This is Muhammad al-Kabir, whom God made stubborn, and I'm just a poor woman who expected that Maryam would be happy because her husband would be coming out of prison. But as I understand it, Muhammad, my son, she had never agreed that Mannan should go to present him with the renunciation document."

"Father," I said to him, "don't complicate the issue. My

brother, Muhammad al-Kabir, has his convictions and is responsible for his own fate."

My father, who didn't really believe things had gone that far, answered, "Wait and see, Mannan!"

Rio de Janeiro
March 7, 1962

My Dear Father,

I received your letter and was glad to hear your news. May God preserve my brother, Muhammad al-Asghar, who writes out your letters to me in his neat hand. A thousand greetings to him from me. Thank you, Father, for sending a picture of yourself and Mother. I looked at the picture and kissed it, and shed tears. Thank you for sending a picture of Fahima and Mannan. How I miss Mannan when I see his face, brimming over with innocence! And how I miss my wife when I see her lovely face and bewitching eyes! It's enough that you understand, Father!

I was glad that the news of my brother Salman and my cousins in Kuwait is also good. Of course, I send them a letter every two months, but my brother Salman's letters are few and far between, perhaps because he's busy in the gas station, may God aid and preserve him. I was really shaken when I learned from you that my cousin Ahmad had not succeeded in finding work there, and that after seven months staying with relatives who had traveled to Kuwait before him, he packed up his bag and went home—repeating some vocabulary in the Kuwaiti dialect, as you mentioned to me, in order to convince his listeners that he really had been in Kuwait. I know Ahmad 'Abbas, he doesn't like wonders or fasting in Rajab, as the expression goes. Anyway, I send him a thousand greetings from here.

I myself am okay, Father, but it is time to stop.

Your loving son,
'Atwan

■

The seventh of June 1962 was a day with special meaning in my life. It was the day I married Sanaa.

We partied in our house for three nights. The people of Ra's al-Naba' arrived in the courtyard, as is the custom at our weddings, and then women gathered in a room in the house. We lit bright lanterns we'd bought from a shop belonging to 'Uthman, my aunt Hayfa's husband. The musicians set up for entertainment, young men started dancing the *dabka* to the tunes of the reed flute, and women danced and sang. The scents of men and women mingled in the air, together with the desire to savor the pleasures of life.

Despite the fact that my brother Falihan had become someone to be reckoned with in Ra's al-Naba' after becoming rich, the yearning for his days as a shepherd had never left him. He brought his flute, which had long accompanied him on the mountain trails as he grazed his flocks, and played it on the wedding nights.

Sanaa had lived with her family in Jerusalem and moved on our wedding day to live with me in our house in Ra's al-Naba'. We brought her in a procession of cars. I sat beside her in one car, then got out and opened the door for her and led her by the hand to the room where the women were gathered.

My father and mother were both happy on our wedding day. My mother danced and sang.

On your wedding day, Muhammad,
twelve taxis at the door of the house...

One letter arrived that I expected my father would not be pleased about. My prediction proved right, for as soon as I read it to him, he appeared obviously irritated. 'Atwan had made the acquaintance of a Brazilian woman, had fallen in love with her, and she with him.

Rio de Janeiro
July 15, 1962

Father, after kissing your hands and asking about your health and the health of my mother, Mathila, and my brothers and sisters, and after congratulating my brother Muhammad al-Asghar on his marriage to Sanaa, this to let you know that I am comfortable in my little house. I can reassure you that my relations with my fellow clansmen couldn't be better, though we are all going our separate ways.

It's true that living alone in my own house has stirred in my soul the desire for a life companion. It's enough that you understand, Father. My God! If only I could bring Fahima and Mannan to live with me. But living expenses here are high, and I wouldn't be able to save any money to send to you. By the way, I changed the equivalent of three hundred dollars and sent them to your address. Please accept this sum from me. God willing, other sums will follow. Father, this is to let you know that I have got to know a young local girl, who works in a food store. I go to the store to buy what I need there, and in time the girl started to recognize me and to smile at me whenever she saw me. Honestly, my acquaintance with her is quite innocent. I am not like the clansmen who get to know Brazilian girls for purposes that are not innocent. Your understanding is enough, Father.

Her name is Giselle. When I mentioned my name to her she smiled and then pronounced my name in a flirtatious manner, *Atwan*, without the initial guttural. I almost leaped from the ground with joy, and to express my respect for her I invited her to my house. She came on her day off and we cleaned the house together. The fact is that she made me feel how close she was to me as she swept the floor, her bare feet soaking in water. I was barefoot as well. Then we ate lunch together. Giselle sends you a thousand greetings, Father, and I send a thousand greetings to you and Mother, and to the family and relatives.

Farewell.

Your loving son,
'Atwan Mannan al-'Abd Al-Lat

My father commented to me one evening, "From the day that 'Atwan traveled to Brazil, we've received one thousand dollars from him. Try to count how many thousands of greetings we've received from him."

My mother Wadha and I laughed. Then she asked God's protection from Satan, the wicked, for she was afraid that the laughter would be followed by some evil lurking somewhere.

Rio de Janeiro
October 15, 1962

Father, I will not hide from you the fact that for some weeks now, I have been wanting to marry Giselle. I dream about her every night. I pick up my bag and walk to the outlying suburbs and see her walking beside me. I will not hide from you that in this country there are young men from our country who squander whatever money they have on worthless things and on chasing Brazilian girls. I don't want to behave like that and I don't want to slander my fellow clansmen here. Please understand, Father. Please reassure my wife Fahima that I won't forget her and that she will continue to have a place in my heart. When I come back to my country she will be my beloved wife, just like Giselle. She can be content, and I very much hope that she will bring up our son Mannan well.

From here, Giselle sends you a thousand greetings, as do the other members of our clan, and a thousand greetings to everyone who asks about us at your end.

Your loving son,
'Atwan

My father didn't object to 'Atwan wanting to marry again. There wasn't anything surprising about that in his eyes. He encouraged it, and saw in it a strengthening of the family's status. And he wasn't irritated because 'Atwan wanted to marry a Christian, for he was fairly open-minded and had no problem with a Muslim marrying a Christian woman. Indeed, he had already experienced my brother Muhammad al-Kabir's marriage to Maryam. He had given his blessing to that marriage and saw nothing strange in it (although the more traditional members of the clan, including my brother Muhammad al-Saghir, certainly did). My father paid them no attention but left them to strut around like frightened cocks. They carried on gossiping and whispering to each other until they became exhausted, at which point they quieted down.

No, the reason my father was irritated was because he believed that, after his wedding, 'Atwan would no longer be sending him money. He was weighing 'Atwan's marriage against the opportunities for receiving money from him, and he found the balance sheet unsatisfactory and not to his advantage. He realized that the money would not come, or if it did, it would be only a few dollars. When 'Atwan traveled to Brazil, my father had set his hopes on an occasional flow of money trickling down on him. He had imagined himself living comfortably, at a time when money was generally scarce. But gradually, my father's irritation lessened, and he was happy whenever a letter arrived. He accepted the situation, and said to me, "Write to him, Muhammad, and tell him that this marriage of his has my blessing."

Rio de Janeiro
December 20, 1962

Really, Father, our wedding was one of the best. I didn't spend too much money, because I am intent on saving it and sending it to you. I invited the members of our clan to the wedding and some Palestinian and Arab friends. Giselle invited her family and some friends, male and female. I rented a hall, where we held the wedding with recorded songs. The music blared and the songs were loud. Giselle's friends danced with their husbands, and her unmarried friends danced with a friend or another guest. Everyone's face looked happy, and I was as happy as could be.

The other clansmen were dancing with Brazilian girls, joking with them, and everyone was laughing. Your understanding is sufficient, father. Then they sang some songs together in Portuguese and also some Palestinian songs, which pleased all the guests, men and women alike. I only danced with Giselle. Everyone who came to the wedding was given a meal, and we left the hall at midnight. Giselle and I went back home. It's a small house, Father, but it's big enough for the two of us.

I send you and everyone who asks about me a thousand greetings from here, and Giselle also sends you a thousand greetings, and a thousand greetings from me and her to Mother.

Your loving son,
'Atwan

My father was even happier when his son told him that he had had his first male child with his Brazilian wife! My father expected the child to be named Mannan, after him, despite the fact that 'Atwan's son by his wife Fahima was already called Mannan. But it seems that my brother didn't like the idea of having two sons with the same name, so he called his son Simon Bolivar.

For a time my father was unable to utter the name of his grandson. He was sure that the name had its origins in the imagination of his Brazilian mother, and he was pleased when 'Atwan informed him in a subsequent letter that the name commemorated a great warrior who had liberated Latin America from colonialism. My father started sending greeting after greeting to his grandson, in letters that I would write to 'Atwan on his behalf, contenting himself with the first part of his name, Simon, which he found easier to pronounce.

■

I opened my notebook and looked over the events I'd recorded. After carefully reviewing all the many incidents, I chose one that had happened to a young woman who had suffered for so long before obtaining a divorce from her wicked husband.

The moment the word "wicked" took shape in my mind, I realized that Tawfik El Deken was the actor to play the part. He would thank me for the confidence that I placed in his talents, because the roles I'd seen him in hadn't included any leads. This time he would be the lead, and naturally, without any hesitation, the heroine would be my beloved Maryam Fakhr al-Din. Maryam, the wife of my brother Muhammad al-Kabir, would be so happy when I told her I was writing a part worthy of the talents of an actress with the same name as her—the daughter of a Muslim father and a Christian mother. And there was another reason to be happy that might remind Maryam of the experience of marriage that she and my brother Muhammad al-Kabir had.

The problem, as I recorded it in my notebook, was that a young man working in a household goods shop had married the daughter of the butcher whose shop was next to his. The girl was respectable and well behaved. The young man—let's suppose his name was Sufyan (not his real name, which is in my register)—used to see Fatin (her real name is also in my register) when she came to her father's shop. She was really beautiful, and every day Sufyan became more and more enamored of her. Fatin noticed that Sufyan kept looking at her pretty face whenever he saw her. She showed that she liked him, and the two young people fell more and more in love. He married her in accordance with the custom of God and His Prophet. Sufyan waited three years, but Fatin did not bear him a child.

Sufyan longed to have a child. His father and mother impressed on him the need to have his wife examined by a doctor to find out why she was taking so long to become pregnant. The doctor confirmed that Fatin was sterile. Sufyan was disappointed and gradually his love for her started to wane. At the same time, his parents were urging him to take a second wife. He gave in to his parents' wishes. Fatin accepted her fate and lived for five years with her co-wife, during which time she experienced misery and humiliation. The second wife gave birth to three children, and Fatin had to hurry to them whenever they cried or complained. Finally, she could bear it no longer. She asked for a divorce and went to court. She praised the Lord when she secured her freedom and went back to her father's house to live a life that still had its downsides, but they were far fewer than those she had experienced in her husband's house.

I began to spend long evenings engrossed in writing, until Sanaa started to grumble about me at certain times of the night. She slept alone in the bed, while I hid away in the living room, with my papers spread out in front of me, writing nonstop, then rereading what I had written and finding that I didn't like it. I would then rip up the pages and rewrite it. I stayed awake thinking about the language that the characters in the film would speak in. Should I use classical Arabic or Egyptian colloquial? I was personally inclined towards classical Arabic because I was of a nationalist disposition and was not in favor of the spread of local dialects that might split the nation and hinder the project of Arab unity for which the leader Gamal Abdul Nasser was now working.

When I pictured Tawfik El Deken playing the part in classical Arabic, I hesitated because I couldn't be sure the actor wouldn't make linguistic errors that might detract from the beauty of the language and get in the way of the dialogue's meaning. But why shouldn't I trust Tawfik El Deken to perform the role in classical Arabic, since he was such a talented actor? How could I allow myself to judge him with no evidence? Then I tried to persuade myself not to put too much stress on the question of language. Abdul Nasser himself, the greatest proponent of unity, gives his own lengthy speeches in Egyptian colloquial. In which case, there is no need for fears about classical Arabic—one way or another, you can get by with local dialects.

I made my decision and started to write the dialogue in

Egyptian colloquial. I wrote some dialogue for Maryam Fakhr al-Din and read it to Sanaa. She listened to the dialogue, then after a few minutes she laughed and asked, "Is this dialogue, Muhammad?"

"What do you think it is, Sanaa?"

"This is a line of a story, Muhammad."

"God forgive you, Sanaa."

I couldn't keep reading and almost gave up writing the script.

One morning, as Sanaa and I got out of bed, she told me that the previous night she had hardly slept at all. She told me that I'd been with Maryam Fakhr al-Din the whole night, talking to her in Egyptian colloquial. For a second time, I almost despaired. I decided to stop writing for the time being, to try and forget Egyptian colloquial and not disturb Sanaa with my public dreams, which might land me in trouble—especially as she knew how much I admired Maryam Fakhr al-Din's acting, as well as her beauty, her delicacy and her sweet voice! I'll go in a different direction for a while, I thought to myself.

■

I followed the 1963 elections for parliament from a distance. The elections came at a critical time. Political activity in the country was banned, and the jails were filled with hundreds of political detainees. My brother, Muhammad al-Kabir, was detained in the al-Jafr desert prison. No one who followed political developments in Jerusalem pinned much hope on the parliament these elections would produce, just as they hadn't pinned much hope on the elections held two years previously. Most of the candidates this time, like last time, were either tribal notables trying to revive the role that had been taken from them by the political parties during the 1950s—merchants with large trade interests, notables from the countryside or regime financiers, including my brother Falihan.

My brother tried to involve me in his election campaign by distributing propaganda for him and making speeches to rallies being staged by agents he had funded. I asked him to relieve me of this task because my work in the sharia court didn't allow me the free time to go around with him giving speeches. I pointed out that the head of the court had advised us not to plunge ourselves into the furnace by engaging in electoral propaganda for the candidates.

My brother shook his head. "I will succeed in the elections despite you and the head of the court."

I promised him that I would vote for him, but I wasn't serious, for I would be betraying my conscience if I voted for a candidate who had sold contaminated milk to people before becoming rich. He mixed it with water, then bought at a discount the low-fat dried milk powder that the UNRWA distributed to the camps and mixed it with goat's milk. He also bought white flour from the Agency, which he mixed with dried milk and sold it to people. Then he turned his attention to smuggling hashish. I went to the voting box and put a blank piece of paper in it. My father went to the voting station and voted for his son, because he was determined, so he told me, to have a son in parliament.

■

Some weeks after I'd stopping writing, I told Sanaa, "I will write the dialogue in classical Arabic."

As my doubts resurfaced, I thought that, despite how much I appreciated his talent, I should propose someone other than Tawfik El Deken to play the part of the hero, because I wasn't confident that he wouldn't make mistakes when he delivered dialogue.

First I thought of Farid Shawqi, but then I hesitated. I didn't think he would feel comfortable accepting this part, a husband hostile to women. I said to Sanaa, "I imagine that Hoda Sultan lives a happy life with Farid Shawqi and that they share their marital home in harmony, which is how she can sing her songs in such a seductive voice. Or so I believe, anyway. Whenever her voice bursts into song, she brings joy to my heart—especially the song, 'If you forget, I'll remind you, how often did my love keep you awake!' Then I said, to Sanaa, "I've found the actor who can play this part—Shukri Sirhan. An actor who can paint his face with all sorts of emotions."

Sanaa replied, "And Maryam Fakhr al-Din, will you exchange her for another actress?"

"No, no, no one but Maryam Fakhr al-Din!"

Sanaa smiled.

"Okay, come on, come to the lunch table!" she said, slightly scornfully.

We ate our lunch, together with Maryam Fakhr al-Din, who was with us at the table.

My relations with Sanaa had reached a crisis point.

"You've started to dream in classical Arabic, in a booming voice," she informed me, adding that if I'd continued to dream in colloquial Egyptian instead, it would have been less annoying. She'd gotten used to hearing a whispering sound, like the chirping of birds, and laughter. But now, with the classical Arabic, things had changed. She heard resounding speeches, and lines of poetry in columns, and sayings handed down to us by our righteous forebears so that we, their descendants, could benefit from their warnings and admonitions.

"I forget that I'm next to you in bed and feel like I'm sleeping in a language institute." She went on, "I even heard Maryam Fakhr al-Din expressing her annoyance at what you were saying and at the part you'd given her and her share of dialogue. I heard her say, 'Give me a break, Hammada! What is this *muga'las* speech that you're writing, my friend?'"

I was amazed by two things. How had Maryam Fakhr al-Din appeared in my dreams with her own voice? And how had Sanaa heard her speaking so freely? Then again, what did this word *muga'las* mean?

This word frustrated me. Was my writing really *muga'las*? I was so embarrassed that I spent several days trying to get Sanaa to explain the word's meaning to me, but she couldn't help. In fact, for some reason she deliberately tried to make sure that the word remained a riddle or puzzle.

Finally, she explained herself without beating around the bush.

"If you insist on continuing to write—either in classical Arabic or Egyptian colloquial—you can keep on enjoying your rosy dreams. But in another room of the house—and in another bed."

Now I understood where things stood. I had two choices.

I could either continue writing, choking on the word that Maryam Fakhr al-Din had spoken in the dream, or stop writing and no longer dream about her and the film, so as to be able to sleep in my wife's bed.

I thought about it for some time. Then I chose the second option, and told her so.

■

Rio de Janeiro
September 10, 1964

Dear Father,

I am writing to you in amazement that the women of the clan have still not stopped gossiping. One of the clansmen received a letter from his family, saying how the women found pleasure only in gossiping about Giselle and spreading rumors about me and slandering me. Without taste or shame, they said that she wasn't a virgin when I married her. They said that before I got to know her, a devil must have slept with her after he saw her in the street wearing the sort of short pants that lead to every sort of sin!

Where did they get this sort of idea from? Who asked them to set themselves up as guardians of Giselle's behavior, or of the clothes she wears? Father, I don't want to comment on this. This is a personal matter that concerns Giselle and me alone. I am not obliged to present a report to the women of the clan about Giselle's past or her present, or to receive their blessings. I didn't have to produce a white handkerchief with Giselle's blood on it on our wedding night. No one asked me for that. Even her family didn't ask for it, and nor did any of my fellow clansmen who are with me in Brazil.

So please teach the women of the clan some politeness when speaking of Giselle, who has become a member of the al-'Abd al-Lat clan. From here I send you a thousand greetings, and Giselle does too. Farewell and peace.

Your loving son,
'Atwan Mannan

After I read this letter to my father, he rubbed his temple for a minute. Then he took the letter from me and hid it in his pocket, instead of leaving it with me as he'd done with 'Atwan's earlier letters. He said, "Can you keep a secret, Muhammad?"

We didn't tell anyone in the family, male or female, about what was in my brother's letter. My father asked me to reply to it in general terms, in a sense saying, "Don't worry, God willing, everything will be fine between you and the clanswomen."

He shook his head and said quietly, "Leave the vessel to travel onward, my son!"

I bowed my head to show my respect. I realized that he still possessed the sort of wisdom that was one of the marks of the clans' sages when they faced difficulties.

That night, I went to bed late. Sanaa was fast asleep.

I dreamt that my father was standing on a piece of high ground from which he could look out over Ra's al-Naba'. He could see a lot of things that didn't please him. He swallowed hard, averted his gaze and kept walking until I thought he would go up to heaven.

Then I saw my mother watching my father and saying to him, "Why do you say nothing, Mannan?" "Silence is a sign of contentment, Wadha," he replied to her. I wondered what is this silence, and what is this contentment, that my father is talking about?

Next, I saw my brother Falihan, who poured his heart out.

I saw him going up the mountain, and I said, "My father's death is near, and if God chooses him to be near Him, I shall mourn him, but I shall become clan leader after him, because I don't believe that my other brothers want to compete with me for this position…My father puts his trust in Muhammad al-Asghar, but I don't believe that Muhammad al-Asghar is thinking of becoming clan leader. Muhammad al-Kabir isn't thinking of it, either. He hardly leaves prison before he's back in again. Muhammad al-Saghir is busy with worship and with calling people to the true religion. The rest of my brothers are engrossed in their own affairs. I will be clan leader, and the government that meets in Amman will agree to install me in the position, as it knows that I am keen to enter parliament. And I, Sheikh Falihan Mannan al-'Abd al-Lat, will serve my family and my clan and the people of Ra's al-Naba', so that high and low will say, "We have never seen anyone like Mukhtar Falihan and will never see anyone like him again."

It occurred to me in my dream to contest Falihan's words, but I found myself unable to speak. Then I saw my father returning from the mountain peak, as if he'd decided to continue living. I called him, but he didn't hear me. My brother Adham joined me, and we started calling him together, but he didn't stop or respond to us. We kept on calling him until I woke up. My brother Adham wasn't with me.

I told Sanaa, who had gotten out of bed before me, that I hadn't slept well and might be very tired that day.

■

When I recalled my dream, I remembered how my brother Adham had been an admirer of Nawal's ever since he had seen her in the market with her fellow students at the beginning of the 1940s, when they were making a trip in the city. He started thinking about her and wanted to get closer to her. He left the hotel where he worked and went loafing around in the markets in the city, her image never leaving his mind. He developed a habit of turning in every direction whenever he wandered through the markets in the hope of meeting her by chance, just as he had done the first time.

Whenever he felt a yearning, he would go to the place where he had seen Nawal and stand there like a humble worshiper, looking at the details of the place and seeing his beloved in every detail. Then he would cross the same road where Nawal had been walking with the school girls. When he didn't find her, he would ask everyone in the family, male and female alike, about the school where she studied. He found out the name of the school and started going there to look for Nawal. Several times he waited near the main gate, watching the groups of school girls coming out like the waves of the sea.

Adham had long ears, like horses' ears. Plus, his eyes were intoxicated and he couldn't tell one school girl from another, for they all looked alike in their blue uniforms and pretty faces and hair hanging down over their shoulders. How could he spot her among all the others when he had only seen her once in school uniform? His whole life was filled with waiting and longing, but he never despaired of reaching his beloved. Finally, he decided to go to the headmistress. He went into her office and said that he wanted to see his cousin, to give her a message from the family. The headmistress looked at him carefully, staring him up and down, suspecting that the young man was harboring some ill-intent for the girl. How could she be sure that he really was the girl's cousin? She asked him to sit down and sent for Nawal.

She came in, and Adham's heart skipped a beat when he saw her coming towards him with her tall, beautiful body. He stood up to greet her, and she came up to him and greeted him. The headmistress felt relieved. Convinced by now that he really was her cousin, she said to him, "Come on, give her your message."

Adham was confused. "My father, Mannan, is missing you and your family, and asked me to contact you to come with your family to Ra's al-Naba," he said.

Nawal shook her head in surprise, and said, "My uncle, Mannan, was in our house only a few days ago and didn't need to send you to communicate a request like this on his part."

Adham blushed, and doubts appeared again in the headmistress's eyes. He couldn't find any way of covering himself, except to say, "That's right, my father asked me to get in touch with you before he came to your house, but I was late in delivering the message."

Nawal knew what Adham's motive must be for coming to the school. The headmistress shook her head and said that the meeting was over.

Nawal went back to her class, and Adham left the school. He didn't stop following her, though. He constantly watched out for her and succeeded in seeing her several times. He approached her and spoke to her, and made clear his warm feelings towards her.

My mother said, "Adham's a nice boy, and Nawal's a pretty and intelligent girl. They're quite suitable for one another. That's my judgment—that's Wadha 'Abd al-Hadi's judgment." My father listened to what she said and approved of it, and it encouraged him to ask for Nawal's hand for my brother Adham.

Nawal wouldn't think of it. She was keen to complete her studies at school and then get a job. She said, "I've been keen on a teaching job ever since Sheikh 'Abd al-Qadir got me to stand in for him to keep the boys and girls in order and teach them songs."

Mathila, my father's wife, and some other women accused Najma of encouraging her daughter to turn Adham down. Najma said, "I didn't encourage her to reject him. That was her decision."

After Nawal had rejected him, my brother Adham started to mock and hold in contempt the customs and values that people upheld in Ra's al-Naba'. He drank alcohol quite openly, while continuing to work in a hotel in the town, where it was said he had short-term relationships with foreign tourists. Then he went to Holland. He told me, "Yes, I went there because I hated this country and its people."

A tourist came to Jerusalem and was staying in the hotel

where he worked. He went into her room to make the bed and clean the bathroom, thinking that she had left the room. She liked the look of his handsome appearance and thought he looked like a real Oriental. She said her name was Claudia and invited him to have a glass of wine.

He had been waiting for a chance like this. Claudia promised that she would help him travel to Amsterdam. That pleased him, and he stopped restraining his voice to please her. She said she liked to hear him neighing loudly.

He stayed with her in Amsterdam and remained there for several years, during which he continued to neigh while she listened. We lost contact with him, and he didn't send any letters to my father. My father continued to suffer and feel regret, hoping that he wouldn't die before he had reassured himself about his son with the long horses' ears.

The lack of news about him reminded me of the difficulty of the task I'd been given.

When Adham came back, he told me he'd become bored after a while and didn't want to continue neighing in Claudia's ear any longer. She'd caught him with another woman, was angry with him and threw him out. My brother could no longer bear being away from home and continued his bad behavior. In the end, though, he could find no other way out except to come back home.

He worked in the old hotel he had worked in before. He came to Ra's al-Naba' during his holidays but only met the rest of the family occasionally. I noticed that he'd been affected by foreign habits. Whenever I saw him I'd visit for just a few minutes, then leave, respecting his desire to be left alone.

9

Muhammad al-Asghar

On the third day of the 1967 war, my aunt Ma'zuza died un-expectedly. She had come to visit the family in Ra's al-Naba' a few days before fighting broke out, then suddenly fell ill and couldn't return to her house in Madaba. Her husband, Sayil, hadn't come with her, and we couldn't tell him she had died. Communications had been cut. We couldn't bury her in the Ra's al-Naba' cemetery, because it was within range of enemy fire, so we buried her quickly in an empty space in the quarter, near the place where the gypsies, my brother Wattaf's in-laws, had set up camp. We buried her without arranging a proper funeral, or even opening a condolence hall for her.

The women of the family washed and perfumed her body and plaited her long hair. The body still retained traces of a youthfulness that defied death. She had felt a pain in her chest, lay down on the bed and lost consciousness. My mother be-came confused and sought help from the other women of the family, who rushed to her and began calling on the prophets and saints to confront the evil lying in wait for the al-'Abd al-Lat family and to drive it far away. They burned incense over her and massaged her arms and legs. How Sayil loved her!

He spoke quite openly about his love for her body. Both the women and men of the family knew how he would bow as she took off her clothes in front of him, then spread her long hair over herself so that only her legs and a small area of her thighs could be seen.

My father Mannan was in grief for his sister. He wept secretly, but no one noticed him crying except my mother Wadha. He asked his Lord to forgive him, for perhaps he felt at the moment of separation that he had been a little hard on his deceased sister. My mother said that Ma'zuza had died from jealousy, and added nothing to that statement.

■

When fighting began on the first day of the war, my colleagues and I were busy working in the sharia court on a number of inheritance and divorce cases. The court hall was crammed full of people. When they heard the sound of gunfire, they abandoned their cases and left the court, except for one husband and wife, and their families, who continued urging the judge to look into their divorce case. The judge requested that the case be adjourned until the war ended. The husband and wife's faces both turned gloomy, and they left the courtroom to live together for a further period of how long I do not know, or for her to live with her family awaiting the divorce. Perhaps she would wait for a chance to improve her husband's mood so that he didn't persist in demanding a divorce, or perhaps he would hope that her mood would improve so that *she* didn't insist on demanding a divorce. The matter remained unclear, and I never found out the details behind it.

The staff all looked into each other's faces, with no need for words. The court manager said, "Let's go back to our homes, and may victory be the ally of the nation." We could tell from his tone that he was optimistic, as if he had victory in his hands, or pocket.

Najma and my uncle 'Abd al-Wadud did not escape the humiliation that ensued when the eastern part of the city fell into the hands of the aggressors. Al-Maghariba Quarter where they were living suffered violence and destruction, and my uncle and his wife were forced to leave the quarter and return to their home in Ra's al-Naba'. Najma left her house in her branch-patterned dress with her hair uncovered, stood at the corner of the house and looked towards Jerusalem. She saw the solidly built Church of the Resurrection and the golden color of the Dome of the Rock and sighed, as if she were grieving for the years she had spent there in al-Maghariba Quarter near al-Aqsa Mosque. She gazed at Jerusalem for a long time then went back inside to shut herself in her house, as if she didn't want to speak to anyone, or anyone to speak to her.

Whenever the women of the family saw her in her patterned dress, they made fun of her between themselves and whispered to each other. "The city woman's appeared! The lady's appeared! She's too important for us. We're no longer on her level!"

They laughed raucously, then hurriedly turned to the subject of her and her daughter Nawal, to begin the ritual of making snide remarks that they loved. They claimed that devils ran behind her to look at her bottom through holes in her dress, which scarcely covered her knees, and that they were quicker than my uncle 'Abd al-Wadud to reach her. Then they would make fun of my uncle, whom Najma bossed around as she liked. They said that she rode him during the night and drove him with a stick during the day. As they carried on laughing, Najma would realize that their laughter was directed at her. My mother said she had seen her crying more than once, that she had tried to ease her pain and cheer her up by relating some news about the desert where Najma had been born and lived for a time.

■

My brother Muhammad al-Kabir had left prison, after eight years. That was two years before the defeat of 1967. But in less than a year he was back in, so when the defeat happened he was again in prison. We would sit talking through the long evenings, and my mother would heap blame on him, saying, "I blame him because he opposed successive governments, and he won't escape their revenge. He needs to look out for himself."

My mother thought that saying this would invite a response from Maryam, my sister-in-law, but in fact, the opposite happened. My mother was surprised by Maryam's attitude. She twisted her lips and said, "I was wrong."

My brother Muhammad al-Kabir didn't find out about Aunt Ma'zuza's death for two weeks, when he and the other political prisoners who had been detained in prison were released. He left the prison and waited for an opportunity to cross the river, which was now under the occupiers' control. He risked the crossing and slipped into Jerusalem, where he found Maryam waiting for him, and his son, Omar. He embraced them and asked God for mercy on his deceased aunt.

My mother cried when he came with Maryam and Omar to our house in Ra's al-Naba'. She greeted him and kissed his brow as she recalled how harsh my father had been to him.

There were tears in my father's eyes as he embraced his eldest son. I embraced him and looked at him with respect, wondering how he had managed to remain in prison without his resolve weakening or his convictions faltering. His wife Maryam had continued to wait for him steadfastly.

My father was shocked and swore that he would only go on the hajj pilgrimage once the al-Aqsa Mosque was liberated from the aggressors. My brother Muhammad al-Saghir asked the Lord to pardon my father, because such a decision would bring ruin upon him in this world and the next, and because it wasn't right to link the performance of religious rituals to worldly circumstances that were subject to fluctuation. He recalled the accusation made by some desert clans that our clan was still influenced by rituals of the period before Islam. He explained his views to my father, but my father would not alter his position.

The shock affected not only my father. Many people were shocked by the defeat and lost their faith both in the Arab project and in Nasser, on whom so many hopes had been placed. Then they were seized by grief when he announced his resignation, which he subsequently reversed under popular pressure.

As a result of the defeat, a number of political forces became active in the country. Many members of the al-'Abd al-Lat clan joined a variety of organizations—Fatah, the two Fronts, the Communist Party, and other groups that had sprung up like

mushrooms in the towns and villages and camps. My brother
Muhammad al-Kabir had been a member of the party for years
and had tried to influence some of his fellow clansmen. He
succeeded with some, and not with others. He was able to send
seven young men from the clan to study in the Soviet Union. My
brother Muhammad al-Saghir didn't like this at all. He found in
it a chance to denounce the party for sending men from the
tribe to the country of infidels, returning to Ra's al-Naba' with
a red stamp that only the Lord of the Worlds could erase. My
brother Falihan found in it an opportunity to play his favorite
tune. He said that the clansmen would spend most of their time
lying on the bellies of Russian women, that the al-'Abd al-Lat
clan would have a branch in Moscow in a few years' time, and
that the clan would start giving birth to blond boys and girls.

My brother Muhammad al-Kabir responded to all this
with smiles and few words. He spoke briefly about the scien-
tific revolution in the country that my brother Muhammad
al-Saghir called the Land of Unbelievers, and told us about
Yuri Gagarin, the first cosmonaut, and about Valentina
Tereshkova, the first woman in space. We shook our heads and
there was a silence, broken only by the clicking of my brother
Muhammad al-Saghir's rosary beads. Finally, he said to my
brother Muhammad al-Kabir, "Like the bald woman who
boasts about her niece's hair." Muhammad al-Kabir laughed,
and the meeting broke up.

I remained faithful to Abdul Nasser's ideas. When I discovered that the defeat of 1967 was just as much a disaster as that
of 1948, I became convinced that there was something wrong
with the thinking in our country, which apparently did not

learn from its experiences or take note of what happened to it, to ensure that the same thing—or something even worse—did not happen again. I decided not to join any party or faction. I kept my ideas and convictions to myself and expressed them openly only when essential—just like any self-confident minor official who believes that his job holds the universe in balance. My father encouraged me to steer clear of politics, a sea that could engulf the most heroic.

As a result of all this political agitation, and the proliferation of different people's convictions and persuasions, the clan experienced some confusion when the political leadership called for a boycott on working for the occupiers. Many workers responded to the call but quickly found themselves forced to work for the occupiers again when they found it impossible to secure alternative employment or sources of income. They had lost interest in rearing livestock, and the ground no longer produced anything that would help them to sustain themselves, so people felt confused and conflicted.

A considerable number of clansmen left to work in Israeli workshops, stores, restaurants and hotels. They received monthly salaries greater than my own, for although I had been employed in the sharia court for years, I and my job were not regarded as in the past. As a result, I started to conduct myself more modestly and behave in a way that more befitted a junior employee. I started not bothering to wear a jacket and tie very often, and instead wore a shirt and pants, blending in with the large numbers of other young workers heading to their jobs in the morning.

I was on the verge of telling my father the truth, that in these new circumstances I wouldn't be able to fulfill his expectations of me, but I was afraid that he wouldn't like what I said, so I chose to keep silent. I was also afraid that my mother would suffer a relapse. She explained the task that my father had entrusted me with as being his legacy, after a long life, and that it was his wish that I take charge of family and tribal affairs to the exclusion of my brothers.

My wife, Sanaa, wasn't interested in the family. She was convinced that it was a natural thing for an extended family to misbehave in the course of growth, so the problem didn't concern her. She was pleased with my going to work in ordinary clothes, saying that always wearing a suit and tie put me on the same pitiful level as the traditional employees with protruding bellies and thick glasses that appeared in Egyptian films. I paid careful attention to what Sanaa said and started to try to stay in tune with the times.

More than once, Sanaa woke me in the middle of the night to tell me, "Muhammad, you are ranting and raving out loud."

My mother said that on several nights she woke my father Mannan. She told him, "Your voice is going up to the skies, with your shouting and screaming." And he told her, "Wadha, I'm dreaming that I'm in a battle on a wide foothill, and my rifle won't fire and the enemy soldiers keep getting closer and firing on me."

And Falihan said to me, "Rasmiyya woke up and looked at me in the darkness, as I was mumbling something or other. She saw that I was in pain, my body dripping with sweat, so she woke me up. I said to her, 'It's a nightmare.' She said to me, 'That's why I woke you up, Falihan.'"

I told Sanaa that the country was exposed to serious dangers. Some people think the occupation will last a hundred and fifty years or more—like when the Europeans occupied it and only left ages later.

Mother worries, "My God, his heart's more delicate than the leaves on a tree, and I'm afraid for him! Mannan, who used to be feared by all, has started to feel miserable for the slightest reason and to worry about everything. He sits on a chair beside the radio and keeps rubbing his white hair. He listens to the radio, but I don't know what he's thinking about, and I've begun to notice that he's not the Mannan of old. Mannan is no longer happy with what he hears, and to relieve the pain that's creeping into him, he avoids news broadcasts, wanders off and is amazed that he's lived all these years. My son Muhammad al-Kabir says that his father has lived his life to the full."

I would say the same about my father. He might have been bitten by a snake while he was in the desert and not been able to continue his journey up until today. He might have been killed by British soldiers or Zionist gangs as he took part in the revolution. He might have been killed by a stray or well-aimed bullet in one of the tribal feuds that the desert witnessed. But he has crossed rough roads and lived cruel days before, and stayed alive. And my mother helped him overcome time's cares.

She said, "I never neglected him. I neglected myself, but I never neglected Mannan. The Lord knows I would bear anything for his comfort and contentment. And I know that the one child of his who did more than any of the others to break his heart was his son Falihan."

10

Falihan

I mentioned to Rasmiyya that her brother Ashraf, her cousin and former suitor Sirhan, and others from the camp now known as al-'Awda, had joined the resistance and smuggled Kalashnikovs and revolvers across the border.

"Okay, but so what, Falihan?" she replied.

I couldn't forget how Sirhan had challenged and disrespected me. One time when he was standing near me he said aloud, intending for me to hear him, "The men of the Jordanian authorities should all put a loaf of bread in their mouths and shut up." I kept silent because the time was no longer my time. But I thought, *Thank you, Sirhan. A loaf of bread in the mouth is better than something else. Yes, I am one of the Jordanian regime's men and not ashamed of it. I've said it openly, afraid of no one. But times have changed, and I have to consider that now.*

I shake my head when I recall that this was in the first days after the 1967 defeat.

Now I'm in this wheelchair, and Sirhan is in an Israeli prison. He's still there and won't leave it. Sirhan wasn't detained because he opened fire on me, but was arrested after he'd undertaken an armed operation against an Israeli patrol. Soldiers surrounded his house in the camp and found weapons. They led him off to prison where they tortured him until he almost died. Then a court sentenced him to life in prison.

Muhammad al-Kabir's son Omar was thirteen when his father was detained by a Jordanian security unit in 1957. When the rest of the country fell into the hands of the Israeli aggressors, Omar stayed for two months. He was confused. Then he joined the resistance, like Sirhan and the others, and when an Israeli security unit came to arrest him, he fled to Amman.

Whenever I feel angry sitting in this wheelchair, I console myself by thinking about my past. But I can't spend all my time recollecting. I sleep in my bed, feel fed up, sit in front of the television, feel fed up again, watch the news, soaps and some other programs. I watched one series called *Wake Up!* about a neighborhood where it was every man for himself, starring Ghawwar al-Tusha, with Abu 'Antar of the twisted mustaches and strapping muscles, Yasin Baqqoush, who strings out his words, Husni al-Burzan, with his enormous body, but gentle as a child, Fattoum Haysa Baysa (Rasmiyya was jealous when she saw me looking at her body with interest, then woke up to reality and said, to tease me, "I know the well and its cover," so I pinched her thigh), and the chief of police, Badri Abu Kalabsha. I started to watch Samira Tawfiq on television, giving up on the radio when I could see her with my own eyes.

Previously, I had only heard her melodious voice. I was keen on her and wished a day would come when I could actually see her. Things stayed like that until I saw her in person at a concert where she was singing her most beautiful songs. I'd gone to Lebanon for a matter connected with Sheikh Za'al's and my business. She sang my favorite song, "You with the White Headdress!" I tried to approach her that evening to shake her hand, but the organizers of the concert—who didn't know who I was or anything about me—stopped me, so I wasn't able to say hello to my favorite singer. I left and the regret has stayed in my heart.

When I saw her on television, I was delighted. I could see the mole on her cheek. I saw her sexy body swaying in her soft dress, which fell down over it. I saw her dark eyes, long eyebrows and black hair. My God, what a great thing television is! Samira Tawfiq was here with me in the house, only steps away. If only she could leave the screen behind and accept my invitation to have supper with me, spend some together, singing, laughing and telling jokes.

But with time, I got bored and tired. I got tired of the news on the radio and the TV programs. In the evening, I didn't hear any songs sung by Samira Tawfiq about love or lovers. Or sometimes the TV broadcast one of her songs when I wasn't watching. "I'm tired," I'd say to Rasmiyya. "Come on, let's go to bed!"

I'd wash the plates and pans and glasses, and make sure that the front door was shut. I would turn off the light in the kitchen and sitting room, and move the chair into the bedroom. She would follow me and shut the door to the room, take off her lilac dressing gown and stay in her nightdress. She'd help me out of the chair to the bed, straighten my legs and stretch them out on the bed. I lay down and she lay down beside me, spreading the cover over our two bodies, then turn off the light at a switch nearby.

I'd stretch out my arm towards her and put my hand under her head. "Sleep on my arm," I would say to her. She'd come nearer to me and her body would cling to mine. "I don't feel like sleeping," I'd say. We'd keep talking and reviving memories.

What I've always liked about Rasmiyya is that she doesn't complain much. She's controlled even when she's happy, and she keeps her feelings noticeably to herself. Whenever I could see that she was in pain for some reason or other, I would ask her what was hurting her, and she wouldn't complain or grumble too much, before going back to her usual easygoing self.

I'm careful to talk to her only about pleasant things, and to relive with her our nicest memories—our days and nights in Ramallah, the concerts we used to attend, the restaurants we used to go to. She enjoys recalling those days and nights, and we stay like that until she gets tired and goes to sleep on my arm. I smell her long, soft hair, unable to sleep, and stay awake with my memories until after midnight.

I've complained about my situation to my brother, Muhammad al-Asghar. He is a civilized man, though several years younger than I am, and I've taken comfort in what he has said. He has a calm temperament and doesn't get angry, harbor grudges in his heart or get annoyed if someone has a difference of opinion with him, or criticizes him for some particular idea or attitude.

I believed he was a Communist, like our brother Muhammad al-Kabir. I suggested that he might have been influenced by him, but he assured me that he did not belong to the party. He said that he was more of a Nasserist. I told him he was free to believe what he liked. I considered myself a royalist, despite the loss of half the Kingdom. I respected him a lot when he said, "Differing views can live together without having to be banished; the field is large enough for all the horses. We just have to train ourselves to be tolerant and accommodating."

I liked what my brother Muhammad al-Asghar said, although I couldn't apply it to myself. I couldn't put up with some of the ugly faces that deserved just to be slapped with a shoe. Of course, I didn't speak openly like this in front of my brother, because he might accuse me of hating people. He came to my house from time to time, and Rasmiyya and I would both treat him hospitably. She would offer him fruit, bring tea after the fruit, then round off the hospitality with coffee.

He would sit and chat with me, and I would feel pleasure in speaking with him, in telling him of the experiences and situations I had been through, and of the challenges and difficulties I had faced. Meanwhile, Rasmiyya would keep her distance, not listening to what I was saying, although a lot of what I was saying to him I had either said to her in the past or would say to her in the future. He listened to me respectfully and valued my journey through life, despite its being tainted by actions and situations he could not accept or support. But he clearly regarded it as a life that would not have been as rich if I hadn't plunged into it, with all the dangers and suffering that went with it.

I spoke to him about the tedium I felt, and he understood how I was suffering. He advised me to read books, because they made our lives richer and more beautiful. I accepted his advice eagerly and recalled what I had learned in the desert at the hands of the sheikhs and preachers. Despite dividing my time then between my studies and looking after the animals,

I was an outstanding student. I had memorized the Qur'an, as well as my addition, subtraction, multiplication, and division tables. I had also memorized a lot of poems, songs and literary texts the preacher had given to us. I had read the *taghriba* of the Bani Hilal and its hero Abu Zayd al-Hilali, and was still interested in it. I had read the story of 'Antara, the story of Zir Salim, and other books.

My brother brought me a book called *The Conference of the Birds*, by Farid al-Din 'Attar. I read a page here and there in a disorganized fashion. I enjoyed a few pages of it, then dozed off. I had no interest in reading it page by page. I was still new to the habit of reading, after giving it up for many years, though I understood that the book is a record of a journey undertaken by the birds to a distant place, led by a hoopoe that explores the horizons. My brother appreciated my attitude and brought me a book by an Egyptian writer, Mustafa Lutfi al-Manfaluti. The book was called *al-'Abarat* ("Tears"). I read it and was affected by the tragedies of the lovers, but I couldn't take all the sighs and pain, chewing over emotions, or the fancy language.

I won't deny that I went through an experience like that when I got to know Rasmiyya and fell in love with her. But I didn't shed tears or spend long nights unable to sleep. And I never lost my appetite because I was unable to join my beloved. Sometimes I felt on edge, or lustful and eager for sex, but never the sighs or pain.

That sort of talk is not in my nature. I like to get to the point, especially with women, without long preliminaries. That's why I seduced Rasmiyya and made her break off with her fiancé, then married her and waited seven days before she let me near her body because she had experienced a shock that made her critical of me. But she got over all this and forgave me. I loved her from the beginning and still love her to this day. Despite that, I never escaped the consequences of my actions, for her cousin never forgave me for what I'd done, and never forgot it. He continued to harbor enmity towards me until he had the chance several years later—the opportunity that made him and all the camps rise up against injustice and submission, as he'd say—and he fired on me.

My brother brought me some books by Naguib Mahfouz, Yusuf Idris, Muhammad 'Abd al-Halim 'Abdallah, and others. I read them all with pleasure. I liked some of them and was unenthusiastic about others. Rasmiyya approved of my love of reading books. She had studied in school for ten years but stopped when the 1948 disaster happened. For some reason, she never enrolled in the school that had been set up in the camp. She started reading with me and liked to talk about what we had read when we were lying in bed together, especially situations involving love and betrayal, as well as explicit scenes that some books contained. She would comment on them shyly, while I would comment on them brazenly, but she wasn't upset by what I said. She listened to me with pleasure, and I would feel that desire had taken hold of her. I would stoke the flames further, then try to contain it and put it out in a way that pleased Rasmiyya and enabled her to sleep quietly, after a long day of anxieties in the kitchen, in the living room and in bed.

My brother brought me a book called *The Epistle of Ibn Fadlan*, describing a journey to the land of the Turks, the Khazars, the Russians, and the Slavs. What caught my eye in it was that Ibn Fadlan and his companions met a Turk and his wife, and sat down to chat with them. While they were chatting, the wife lifted her dress and exposed a part of her body that should not be exposed in public. The travelers and those with him were confused and tried to avert their gaze from what they had seen, but the wife paid no attention; as far as she was concerned, it was all quite normal and not something to cause confusion. The husband tried to clarify matters for Ibn Fadlan and his companions by saying that it was better to expose it and preserve it than to hide it from sight and then make it available to others.

This reminded me of Rasmiyya's underclothes before I married her—before I asked her not to wear them, but instead to wear the short ones that the women of Ra's al-Naba' used to buy from the stores in Jerusalem, after they'd stopped sewing their own from cheap cloth. I was seized by a renewed curiosity to know why Rasmiyya and other women in some regions of Palestine wore this long underwear that they sewed with their own hands from cloth of various colors. What were the circumstances that had made it necessary and prompted them to do it?

I thought that it might have been the influence of the environment on people's customs and habits in dress and food. I took my sister Falha as an example, when she was living in her husband Nu'man's village of al-Wasmiyya and was forced to wear long underwear, in conformity with the prevailing fashion there. Then I thought that maybe it was a desire to impose extra modesty on women. But long *thobs* should be enough to achieve a sufficient degree of modesty. Then I thought that it was perhaps a desire to keep women's bodies warmer. I rejected this explanation because the women wore them in summer as well as winter. If wanting to keep warm had been the motivation, women wouldn't have worn them in summer but would have worn something a lot shorter, so as to moderate the heat and humidity, as well as their body temperature. Then I thought that it might be a desire to surround the sensitive part of a woman's body with an expansive garment so that it would be impossible to reach it as easily. I felt confused, but found by experience that Rasmiyya's clothing only held out for a few seconds when I stormed her body in the desert and found that she wasn't wearing a bra—when I stripped her dress from her body and her breasts were free as two young doves.

I asked her about it but didn't get any explanation or interest in the question. She said that bras weren't common in her village, that her mother, sisters and the girls of the village all wore long underwear, so she had done the same. Her family had made her wear them since she was small, and she hadn't found anything wrong in that, or that invited questioning.

I said it's obvious that these underclothes are connected with farming, where a woman works in the fields just like a man and is forced to lift her long *thob* up over her legs and tuck the two ends under her belt during work hours—the same way that a man lifts his *kumbaz* off his legs to tuck the two ends under his belt. But in that case, it's not right for her to expose her legs. Long underclothes for a woman, like those for a man, are the solution. Then again, if she's climbing trees to pick fruit, she'll be spared the spying of the curious if she is wearing long underclothes.

"Maybe," Rasmiyya replied simply, in an attempt to evade my tedious explanation. I touched her hair and smiled at her, and she smiled back.

I blamed myself for keeping quiet when some people with an obvious self-interest accused me of exploiting others. If I had spoken out and responded more firmly, in a way that brought those who had slandered me to the attention of officials, I might have escaped what Sirhan did to me. After the 1967 defeat, it was said that a new spirit had entered the camp. As he prowled around the alleys of the camp, Sirhan said, "The time for surrender is past."

It seemed strange for him to be saying this now. After the 1948 disaster, Palestinians faced humiliation and subjugation. Hundreds of thousands were dispersed and became refugees in camps. That disaster was as bitter as the 1967 defeat, so why was the time now past for surrender? Of course, I was not opposed to ending the time for surrender. In fact, I couldn't accept that the camp should live in a state of surrender. I had to be wary of Sirhan, but he fired at me with a revolver, which it had been difficult for him to get hold of before.

My brother Muhammad al-Asghar tried to explain what had happened. "As the resistance penetrated the camps and elsewhere," he said, "the camps woke up and started to rebel against the conditions they had been forced to live under in the past." That was what my brother kept saying, though it went against my own convictions. And that was what Sirhan thought, and proclaimed publicly. So his old anger towards me awoke. He said that he would take vengeance for the honor I had dragged through the mud. He opened fire on me as I left my sister Falha's house on the edge of the camp. It was fortunate that my sister and brother-in-law immediately came to my assistance.

My mother Mathila said my father suffered because of what had happened to me. She told me,

Your father became an object of hate, although he tried not to appear guilty in front of others. He started raving at night, saying things like "I, Mannan Muhammad al-'Abd al-Lat—my son Falihan has been shot by one of the fedayeen! I took part in the 1936 revolt, and I am the father of two martyrs, Wattaf and Yusuf." He started talking about the years his son Muhammad al-Kabir spent in prison, recalling how he was mukhtar of the clan in the time of the Mandate and the period of Jordanian rule, and how he had refused to continue as mukhtar after the 1967 defeat. A few weeks after the defeat, he threw down the mukhtar's official seal in the office of the Israeli military governor and left with no regrets. He was tormented because people had no mercy. Some people said that Falihan was an agent of the occupiers, and this was the thing that hurt your father's heart the most.

In one of his letters, my brother 'Atwan said, "Honestly, Father, I was greatly affected when I found out what had happened to my brother Falihan. The clansmen here in Brazil are all affected."

I know that my father was unhappy about some of my behavior—dealing in hashish and smuggling goods to the enemy state. But he knew full well that I was incapable of betraying my conscience and becoming an agent of the occupation. My brother Muhammad al-Asghar asked his mother Wadha to continue looking after Mannan, because what had happened to me wasn't easy to cope with—for his son to be fired on and not ask the clan to take revenge on anyone, or call upon them to respond to Sirhan. I explained to my father that there was no need to call upon the clan.

My brother Muhammad al-Asghar agrees with me that the situation has changed. Despite the fact that what Sirhan did can be classed as revenge for a family matter, and is unconnected with the national interest, the fact that he has joined the resistance makes things more complicated. I am simply saddened by Rasmiyya's tears. She has taken on the personality of Jalila, the sister of Jassas and wife of Kalib, when her brother killed her husband and left her sad and tormented for a long time.

My brother Muhammad al-Asghar added something else, which might explain why the family affair that had continued to wound Sirhan had become so intertwined with the national question that the two had become inseparable. I had observed how my brother Salman's arrival from Kuwait across the river in secret had apparently obscured what had happened to me, since the clan had been preoccupied with his arrival for several weeks.

My brother Salman had come back from Kuwait before, some months before the 1967 defeat. It was easy for him to reach Jerusalem; there were no obstacles. He came laden with gifts—shirts, pants and ties for the young men, pieces of cloth and silver bracelets for the women, and dresses and perfumes for the girls. He brought my father an embroidered cloak like those worn by the emirs in Kuwait, which my father wore with great pride. He brought gold bracelets and silk kerchiefs for his mother Samiha. My father asked for the hand of his brother 'Abbas's daughter for him, and it was agreed that they should be married in a year.

Then the defeat happened, and Salman was no longer able to return home because the borders were closed. But he came undercover to marry his cousin and take her back to Kuwait. He relied on an experienced guide who knew the area well, and he had several other people with him. He crossed the river by means of a rope stretched from one bank to the other. Luckily for him and those with him, the enemy soldiers didn't see them as they made their way across the river. But when an armed patrol passed close to the border, Salman and his companions were forced to hide among the shrubs growing there.

This time, Salman reached Ra's al-Naba' with a pale face and dirty clothes. His mother Samiha ululated and my father Mannan wept. Salman married his cousin without any singing and dancing, because the country was steeped in blood and because I was still suffering from the blow that Sirhan had inflicted on me. Salman took his bride across the border back to Kuwait. The invaders made it easy for those wanting to leave, providing them with special buses for that purpose. Salman and his bride boarded one of these buses and left the country for an unknown time.

In this way, Salman's sudden arrival was added to the clan's unwritten history. Since that time, the country has not been quiet, and it seems it never will be.

■

I became quite nervous about Omar and Fazza'. When I switched to the Amman channel on TV, all the songs were dedicated to the homeland, to the King and to the men with the red keffiyehs. Fazza', my aunt Ma'zuza's son, belonged to this group, and I was fond of him. I had met him several times before the 1967 defeat. I used to go to Amman and make a diversion to Madaba to visit my aunt and have lunch in the house of her husband Sayil, who swore to divorce his wife if I left his house before he had offered me a feast. He slaughtered an animal and invited a number of men of his clan to greet me and sit with me to eat lunch.

I met Fazza' as well when he came to Ra's al-Naba' with his mother to visit the family. I noticed that he was very intelligent and alert. He joined the army when he turned eighteen, came to the West Bank and took part in the war that ended in defeat. His mother, Ma'zuza, died during the war, and he didn't learn of her death until later. He had withdrawn with the soldiers of his battalion on the fifth day after fighting had broken out, after the balance had turned against them. Fazza', my cousin, and all the soldiers who were with him, were unable to resist the tanks and aircraft, and discovered that their ammunition—or at least, some of it—was defective. They aimed their rifles at the enemy positions and fired. There were ringing noises, but they were nothing more than noises.

Fazza' spoke about it later. He said he expected that there would be an inquiry. How had the defective ammunition come into the soldiers' possession? But there was no inquiry, nor anything else.

I will never forget how, when the battles of September 1970 broke out, I could not sit still, day or night. Rasmiyya couldn't sit still, either. She sat near me, sometimes resting her head on my shoulder, then getting up and coming back with a tray with a teapot and glasses on it. "Lord, be kind!" I said. Omar, the son of my brother Muhammad al-Kabir, is with the resistance in Amman. And Fazza' my cousin is a soldier in the army. I'm hearing news of clashes between the army and the resistance, and my hand is on my heart. My brother Muhammad al-Kabir criticizes the excesses of the resistance but puts responsibility for the clashes on the regime. That's my brother's nature, my brother's politics, always blaming the regime. I tell him, now is not the time to criticize and he asks disparagingly, "Then when should we criticize, if not now?"

Rasmiyya comes into the living room, bringing coffee and tea from the kitchen. I have the radio next to my ear all day and follow Amman TV during the evening until the programming closes with the royal greeting. Rasmiyya says, "Tell me, Falihan, if they agree on a ceasefire," and I reply, "I will tell you, Rasmiyya, for sure!"

I could see that a ceasefire would come into force only after much effort. In fact, Arab interventions and pressure from Gamal Abdul Nasser played a part in stopping the fighting, and Yasir Arafat left Amman secretly.

Sometimes I would sit with my father to chat and pass the time of day. We liked to recall our connections with the leaders. My father continued to want to meet Arafat and Nasser. But Abdul Nasser died and Arafat was in Beirut.

Some weeks after the revolt of 1936 broke out, my father had met the Mufti Hajj Amin al-Husseini. He also met King Abdullah at the Jericho Conference that resulted in the unification of the two Banks, then met King Hussein in the Raghadan Palace to congratulate him on succeeding to the throne. Three years before the 1967 defeat, he met Ahmad Shukeiri at a conference in Jerusalem that resulted in the founding of the PLO.

I met King Hussein when I went with a delegation of the Ra's al-Naba' clans to swear allegiance to him after the chaos caused by the political parties in relation to the country's security. I met Shukeiri before the 1967 defeat in a crowded meeting, though we did not speak to each other. I never met Arafat or Nasser. When I stood for election in 1961 and 1963, I stood with the regime, but people deserted me and did not support me. I left my father's guest house and went back to recollecting those days, saying to my wife, "I failed to be elected, Rasmiyya—I failed twice."

"And what made you think of that, Falihan? That was years ago!"

"You should have cautioned me not to put myself up for election. I spent so much money!"

"If I'd have advised you, you wouldn't have taken any notice!"

"If you want the truth, I blame my brother Muhammad al-'Asghar and the men of the al-'Abd al-Lat clan!"

"That's the end of it, Falihan, try to forget it!"

"Listen, when one of the candidates lost after spending a lot of money, he said, 'You waverers, you ate my wealth and elected someone else!'"

Rasmiyya laughed and expressed surprise at my insistence on recalling that loss, which continued to sting me. I had emerged from the battle of the elections a wounded man. After all the pomp and ceremony, and after all the money I had spent, I came out the loser, and I went back to Rasmiyya almost exploding with anger.

Rasmiyya, as usual, confirmed her decency. She embraced me as if I were a child. She stroked my head, kissed my brow and chest and every pore in my body, until she almost made me forget the pain of losing. I didn't let her go. I stripped her naked and clung to her. It seemed I wanted to empty my feelings of anger, frustration and loss in a headstrong act that did not know how to wait. And I achieved it through Rasmiyya's bewitching body, which turned those feelings into an overwhelming pleasure that made its way sensuously through the cells of my own body.

I would have faced the hardest of tests if my brother Muhammad al-Asghar hadn't encouraged me to read books. From anger, I would have ended my life with a sip of poison. I hadn't read anything except pamphlets by sheikhs and preachers for six years. Had it not been for my experience of life, my acquaintance with all sorts of people, and my intelligence—which my brother never denied—I wouldn't have been able to get to where I did.

I could have been a member of the Jordanian Parliament. I could have been a minister in the government. But fate intervened, and my dreams of securing an important position came to nothing. I might have gotten what I wanted if we hadn't been taken by surprise by the occupation, which threw the course of our lives into confusion. If the occupation and defeat hadn't happened, I would have escaped Sirhan's vengeance and continued on the course of my life as one of the most prominent men in Ra's al-Naba' and the whole region of Jerusalem. I could have continued to expand my influence from one end of the land to the other.

My feelings are aroused, and I recall the *taghriba* of the Banu Hilal and the struggle of the horsemen, led by Abu Zayd al-Hilali and Dhiyab ibn Ghanim. I take up my *rebab* and lift up my voice in song.

> *Abu Zayd al-Hilali Salama says:*
> *A young man's honor is like delicate glass*
> *I protect it from the wicked, who will not break it,*
> *And I do not fear the virtuous*

I play and sing the verses more vigorously, hoping that Rasmiyya will hear me, come closer to listen to me, and ask me to let her hear something of the *taghriba* of the Banu Hilal, as I used to do in the past. But since the television entered our house, she's no longer interested in the *taghriba* or playing the *rebab* or listening to poetry. Instead she seems tied up with something with the neighbors.

I continued to think about where I'd ended up. My ambitions had now receded and I had fewer dreams. I could no longer be bothered to go to inspect the businesses I owned. I no longer had any interest in going to the quarry, which was not producing enough to pay the wages of the workers there. The members of the clan who worked in the café and other shops complained of the high taxes that the occupiers imposed on them and about the small income that these enterprises generated. They were robbing me, but what was to be done? And how could I put things to right? I was no longer willing for people to see me as a cripple in a wheelchair, unable to move unless one of my sons, or Rasmiyya, pushed it if I was distressed and in a critical situation.

What I like about my brother Muhammad al-Asghar is that he doesn't treat me with pity. If I felt for a single moment that he pitied me, I wouldn't have confided or put my trust in him, and I wouldn't have told him all the personal experiences and events in my life.

In a letter that my brother 'Atwan wrote my father Mannan, he said, "Father, I pity the state that my brother Falihan has come to. I was expecting that he would end up like this, as he himself pitied no one—not even me, his brother. He cheated me at work with the salary I received. But still, a thousand greetings to him from me."

'Atwan's words angered me, though with time my anger cooled.

I had greeted Wadha, my father's wife, when we met in my father's guest room a few days before, and tried to improve relations between us. "My father's wife," I said to her, "I love you as I love my mother Mathila."

I saw her face register a reaction, which I reckoned was because she hadn't expected me to say that. She replied saying something about how a pure heart bore no grudges. I knew that my brother 'Atwan, who was my full brother, wanted vengeance on me. He had traveled to Brazil feeling angry at me.

My brother Muhammad al-Asghar told me more than once, "Falihan, my brother, I hope that the books I am bringing you get into your head. Then they can interact with your emotions and change your behavior towards other people, be they near or far away."

"Muhammad," I said to him, "I have my issues with other people, and I have my feelings. I'm no angel, brother, please understand me. I am Falihan ibn Mannan."

11

Muhammad al-Asghar

My brother Falihan has an unpredictable nature. He's silent un-less absolutely necessary, and when he speaks, doesn't say much. He is cloaked in mystery, tinged with cunning betrayed by his eyes, combined with a guile that cannot be mistaken. Many times I've rescued him from sorrow as he sat in his wheelchair, day and night. I did it to try to civilize a spirit sunk in evil.

In his youth, he tried to ravage a girl who was grazing her family's animals in the desert. He attacked her and ripped her *thob* from her chest. Her breasts could be seen by everyone. I hit him with a rock, which split his head open, and she took advantage of his confusion to run away, screaming. When she reached her clan's campsite, dozens of young clansmen raced to the grazing ground to kill Falihan, but they couldn't find him. My father hurried to the Rabahna clan and asked them to inter-vene between our clan and the Rawajfa clan. Before anything could be done to sort things out, a number of young Rawajfa men came to a position close to our clan's tents and fired their rifles at the camp, then went back to where they had come from.

My father went to the al-Aqsa Mosque with a number of our clansmen. He stood in front of a group of people and swore by God that the girl's honor was intact and that his son Falihan had not damaged her. Five of my father's brothers and sons undertook to vouch for his statement on oath. So when my brother Falihan had had his innocence confirmed, my father made a great feast for the two clans, the Rawajfa and the Rabahna, attended by a large number of guests.

Even so, Falihan is not devoid of virtue or intelligence, as he has absorbed a lot of what he reads. He was interested in reading books a long time ago, he said, but had stopped reading when making money became his main interest. His present economic circumstances are no longer the same as they were. His income from his commercial stores has fallen since the 1967 defeat. The quarry that used to provide him with an income to compensate now lacks clients because of the poor quality of the stones that have started to emerge from the mountain rock. When my brother was no longer able to pursue his private affairs as usual, I urged him to read, and he didn't hesitate to accept my advice.

If I am being generous towards my brother Falihan, it was my brother Muhammad al-Kabir that was generous to me, because he got me to enjoy reading. I would visit him in his house after I finished school and sit in his small sitting room. Maryam would bring me tea and a plate with cake on it, and I would eat the cake and drink the tea. My brother Muhammad al-Kabir would give me pamphlets, which he said the party was continuing to distribute to educate the workers, poor peasants, laborers and marginalized people, to make them aware of their rights and save them from exploitation.

That was after the parliamentary elections in which the Party's candidate was successful in Jerusalem. My brother Muhammad al-Kabir and his wife Maryam were proud to have played a part in his winning the highest number of votes. I expected that my brother would be eager to involve me in the Party. I hid the leaflets and pamphlets that he gave me in my school bag, as he impressed upon me the importance of reading them. I read some of them and didn't read others, especially when they were printed in small fonts.

But my brother's enthusiasm for party propaganda didn't last. The security forces raided his house and detained him, and he was sentenced to imprisonment with hundreds of his colleagues, most of whom received severe sentences. I had to bear the burden of my brother in prison, and also the burden of my brother Adham.

Some months after my brother Adham's return to the country, the 1967 disaster took place. He then spent all his time on the streets of Jerusalem chasing Israeli women dressed in clothes that revealed more than they hid. He didn't attract any attention from them. In fact, his approaches to some of them exposed him to scorn and ridicule, since he belonged to a defeated people who didn't deserve to find favor with them, or they would be going against the way they had been taught. They had been brought up to believe that the Palestinians were dirty and treacherous, and were of a lower status than the Israelis, who had been victorious in every war.

When he despaired of them, he turned to Israeli whores, for whom an Israeli was no better than a Palestinian, and vice versa, except insofar as one of them might pay more money.

Adham applied himself to them with something like a mania. Perhaps that was a compensation for the awareness of having been defeated by the Jews, who had come to Jerusalem from every corner of the earth, and who were standing on the thresholds of Palestinian homes, which had become for them spoils of war. Whenever they saw a Palestinian coming to reclaim his house, they taunted him with hollow boasts of how their army had won a stunning victory in the last war over three Arab armies, and how the soldiers of the "Defense" forces had fought valiantly, which had caused the Arab soldiers to flee like rabbits. Adham became furious whenever he heard this sort of thing repeated by hotel guests who came from all over the world on short visits (by permission of the conquerors), to see their cities and houses that had been lost. He was overwhelmed by a desire to get into a battle of a personal kind, whose battleground would be the bodies of Israeli whores. But his battle was lost from the start. It wasn't the whores who were concocting elaborate lies about the heroes of an army that had won a quick victory for some reason, or planning the policies of the state that had been founded, all of a sudden, on the ruins of Palestinians.

Then he was detained as a result of a scuffle with some Israeli youths who couldn't bear to see him embracing an Israeli whore and walking with her to the bar. In prison, he got to know some *fedayeen*, as he told me later, and was influenced by them and by what they had to say about the homeland, sacrifice, and resistance. He left prison, only to go back to it after he had started to smuggle arms into the country. He was arrested for that and sentenced to jail for twenty-three years.

Rio de Janeiro
September, 25 1967

Father, I felt shocked when this disaster happened. All the Palestinians here felt shocked. We believed that Nasser would liberate Palestine. Anyhow, I hope you are well, and that everyone in the clan is in good shape. I hope God will help you overcome this occupation.

My wife Giselle sympathizes with you. My son, Simon Bolivar, is always asking me, "Where is Palestine?" I explain to him and teach him some words in Arabic. The members of the clan send their greetings. They talk to the Brazilians about the tragedy of our people. But they also spend a lot of time joking, and your understanding is sufficient, Father.

I had been thinking of coming to visit you with Giselle and Simon Bolivar. I said that Giselle should get to know her husband's family. I'd spoken of you so much that she was eager to see you. I said I would visit you and kiss your hands and Mother's hands, and reassure myself about my brothers and sisters and about all the members of the al-'Abd al-Lat clan. This would have been a chance for Giselle to visit Jerusalem. She would be happy when she entered the Church of the Resurrection and the al-Aqsa Mosque. And your grandson, Simon Bolivar, would be happy to meet you and speak a few words of Arabic.

But after the fall of Jerusalem into the hands of the invaders, Giselle and I made a pledge that we would only visit after the invaders had been expelled. Instead of visiting, we are spreading the message about Palestine and its people. Giselle is holding meetings to protest against the occupation that are attracting both men and women who sympathize with the Palestinian people. Giselle gets up in the morning dreaming of Palestine and goes to bed dreaming of it. I have taught her our national anthem, and our son, Simon Bolivar, has also learned it. We have started to sing it whenever we meet in one of the squares with a group of Palestinians and Arabs and Brazilian friends. I can tell you, Father, that Simon Bolivar has joined a football club, to train for the game from an early age. Giselle and I have joined a charitable organization for the protection of orphans, and we go there in some of our spare time.

I kiss your hands and those of Mother, and from here I send you and her a thousand greetings. A thousand greetings also to Muhammad al-Asghar.

Your loving son,
'Atwan

■

When we came back from seeing the doctor, my mother couldn't believe that Sanaa didn't know the truth, and my father continued to waver between believing it and not. My mother thought that Sanaa's first husband only divorced her because he discovered that she was infertile and began to look at Sanaa suspiciously, convinced that the barren woman had perhaps been possessed by a devil or a jinn, which would prevent her from conceiving. That would be a bad omen for the al-'Abd al-Lat family, as the malady might spread to other women of the family, so she would have to take the precautions necessary to contain it.

In that case, divorce or taking a second wife would be the least bad solution. My mother didn't know how to persuade me to do what she wanted, and she saw in my apparent stubbornness a bad sign. This stubbornness was an insult to the family destiny and to my personal destiny, because I would grow old over time with no son of my own to lead me along the road, or daughter to wash my clothes and hand me the medicine box.

Sanaa felt humiliated. She said this was not a reason that led her and her first husband to separate. She said he had insisted on postponing having a family for five years because he wanted to enjoy a relationship with his wife unencumbered by the noise of children. At the time, Sanaa had not been aware that she was infertile, and she hadn't misled me.

I believed every word Sanaa said, for she was not the sort to mislead others. But my mother didn't believe her; she was convinced that she had played a deceitful game with me. My father remained doubtful, insisting that I should take a second wife so that I could have a son to inherit from me after my death.

Sanaa didn't object to my taking a second wife, but she made her position perfectly clear—"I will not live with a co-wife." She said that in this situation she would prefer to divorce. I hate even uttering the word "divorce." I couldn't bear to hear it after all my experiences working in a sharia court, and never for a single moment had I thought of separating from Sanaa. Then again, I had experience with the problems of second wives and knew that many cases of divorce that I had seen were because of polygamy. My life was turned upside down as I struggled with my desire to keep Sanaa, and my father and mother's wish to impose a second marriage on me.

My brother Muhammad al-Kabir supported me, and spoke to me in a way that confirmed the need to side with Sanaa's point of view. His wife, Maryam, took the same view, so that my mother, may God forgive her, accused my brother Muhammad al-Kabir of simply saying what Maryam dictated to him. She whispered to me, "Your brother's neck is in a halter and the other end is in Maryam's hand." She also warned me quietly, "Be careful, and don't let Sanaa put a halter on your own neck, my son!"

I stomached her words as I followed news of my brother Muhammad al-Kabir, who'd been detained by the occupiers a year after the 1967 defeat. He said, "In prison I found many detainees."

He remained there for nine months. When they released him, he told us about a lot of things he'd seen and experienced during the inquiry. The evening following his release, he told us about Qasim Abu 'Akar, a Jerusalemite, whom the investigators had continued to torture with electric shock and repeated beatings with a club to his head, until he died. My brother mentioned similar acts of heroism under torture that he had read about in books and pamphlets. On a lighter note, my brother Falihan expressed his wish that the second group of clansmen who had been sent by my brother Muhammad al-Kabir to study in the Soviet Union should not spend too much time with blonde Russian women, but instead should devote themselves to learning, in the hope that those specializing in medicine would return to Ra's al-Naba' with a cure in their pockets for his problem, which had deprived him of the pleasure that God has planted in our bodies.

We talked until we felt we'd had enough. Then we split up and each went his separate way, certain that we'd meet and talk again.

12

Muhammad al-Asghar

My brother Muhammad al-Kabir was employed as a waiter in the Ambassador Hotel in the Sheikh Jarrah district, serving food to the restaurant patrons. While working he would recall previous restaurants at which he had worked in Jaffa and Jerusalem. In the blink of an eye he would review his life, which had not been easy, and how he might have remained only semiconscious had it not been for the appearance of Maryam in his life, who had guided him to new ways of thinking.

Maryam worked in a shop that sold stationery and books. She was amazed at how she had been able to gain Muhammad's confidence in her ideas, which she learned from her brother Ilyas. At first, Muhammad wasn't prepared to discuss things and was rather unsociable and ill at ease. But as he became more attracted to Maryam, he began to listen to her more receptively. After a time, she felt she had rescued a man who might easily have gotten lost in the ocean of life and its clashing waves.

Maryam talked about all this without any sense of weariness and seemed happy with what she had achieved. "Yes, happy," she said, "despite the many years of torment that Muhammad and I both suffered because of his detention."

In years past, my brother had read nothing except for the Party's secret publications. When he was certain that his detention in al-Jafr desert prison would be a long one, he turned his attention to reading books.

I read a lot, including Naguib Mahfouz's *Trilogy*, and I liked it. I liked the character of Ahmad 'Abd al-Jawwad and saw in him some of the same qualities as our father Mannan. I liked the character of Amina and saw in her our grandmother Subha. I read Mahfouz's novel *The Beginning and the End*. I was keen to follow the fate of a family torn apart by the complexities of life after their breadwinner had died. How had the eldest brother Hasan become a thug? And the sister, Nafisa, a whore? And the brother, Hasanein, a police officer? He had some bourgeois attitudes that fed in him an egoistic sensitivity and a concern for his personal interests, so that when he discovered that his sister was a prostitute, the world turned black in his eyes and he forced her to end her life. She threw herself in the Nile, but then he did too, after failing to find any way out except suicide.

My brother told me that while in prison, after he'd finished reading the novel, he started thinking about our own family and what our sister Falha had done. He said he respected Uncle 'Abd al-Jabbar's behavior for not sacrificing her when he rediscovered her after her long disappearance. He also commended our father for forgiving Falha and asking us all to forgive her because she had married the man she loved.

■

Rio de Janeiro
September 12, 1968

Father, on today's date ten years ago, I boarded the airplane from Kalandia Airport and traveled to Brazil. I haven't seen Ra's al-Naba' or Jerusalem since then, and I haven't had the privilege of seeing you and kissing your and Mother's hands.

It's true, I didn't notice the anniversary. It's Giselle who noticed it and said that we must celebrate. I asked her how, knowing the circumstances in Jerusalem now, we could celebrate? But she continued to insist. She said we should invite some Brazilian friends and turn it into an opportunity to remind people that Jerusalem has fallen under occupation, and that we have to stand in solidarity with her and her Palestinian citizens. She said that this commemoration was essential for our son Simon Bolivar, to understand the details of his father's life. I was touched, Father, and tears almost sprang to my eyes as I imagined your grandson Simon growing up in a foreign land knowing nothing of his father's history before he came to this country, or of his grandfather Mannan or his people. He no doubt knows a lot of trivial things, but he still needs more information. But my biggest joy will be when the country is liberated and I can come with Giselle and Simon to visit Palestine and enjoy seeing you and the country.

If you wonder about me, I am well, though I am tired from work. Here, no one eats unless he works and exhausts himself and sweats a lot.

I kiss your hands and Mother's too. Giselle and I send you and Mother a thousand greetings, and from our son Simon Bolivar a thousand greetings to his grandfather Mannan and his grandmother Mathila. Greetings and farewell.

Your loving son,
'Atwan

■

My brother Muhammad al-Kabir left the Israeli prison but stayed in Jerusalem. He said, "Yes, I have left prison and am happy to have escaped its walls, which trouble the soul, but at the same time I am sad for those comrades who are still there."

Maryam suggested to him that he open a kiosk selling books, newspapers and magazines. The idea appealed to him, and he found in it some physical comfort after his previous hard life, as well as a chance to express his love for books. So he opened the kiosk and started selling books, newspapers and magazines. When he didn't have any customers, he absorbed himself in reading. "That's right," he said, "and I've developed links to intellectuals and journalists in the city. They gather around me, and I have conversations with them about culture. Afterwards, we talk about Jerusalem and its fate. We have differing views, but I don't try to impose my ideas on anyone."

When my brother found out that a theater troupe had appeared in Jerusalem, he became enthusiastic about it and started to follow its progress. He and Maryam hurried to visit its headquarters in the Sheikh Jarrah district, to encourage it and get some people together to follow its performances. He got to know the troupe's director and other actors there. Then he invited me and Sanaa to attend one of their performances on the stage of the Omariyya School in Jerusalem. I hesitated a little on account of my work in the sharia court, and because I was a sharia registrar. I almost excused myself and wouldn't have gone, were it not for the insistence of Sanaa, who thought it quite natural that I should go to the theater, without any concerns.

We went and our emotions were rocked as we watched the troupe's acting! My brother Muhammad al-Kabir said that he and Maryam too were moved when they saw the performance, which could be interpreted as an invitation to resist backwardness, or to resist the occupation—or both. He said that they were reminded of Khalil al-Sakakini, an educator who was one of the leading proponents of enlightenment in the city, and in Palestine. Maryam cried a lot, he said, when Sakakini died in Cairo, far from Jerusalem and from his home in al-Qatmoun Quarter, which had been conquered by the Zionist occupiers. He said that those working in the theater troupe represented a natural extension of al-Sakakini, Ruhi al-Khalidi, Kulthoum 'Awda, Nasri al-Jawzi and others. He said that Maryam admired the only actress in the troupe and thought her a brave pioneer, because she was happy to appear on stage at a time when Jerusalem women were, unfortunately, reluctant to take part in the theater.

"Wow!" I said to Sanaa after watching the performance.

"What did you find, Archimedes?" she replied.

I smiled at her teasing and pledged, "I will write a play for the troupe."

Sanaa thought about it. "That would be great!"

"Yes, I will write about women in our society and the injustices done to them.

"I will write a part for the only actress in the troupe using my experience in the sharia court and entrust the part of the sharia registrar to the actor who played the intellectual gossip, because his performance was so skillful and convincing. I think that the audience will applaud a lot. Tears of joy will fall from my eyes as I see my role as a sharia registrar being played by a distinguished actor. It will be a brilliant performance, my words on his tongue and taking shape on the stage."

I told Sanaa I would check her expression from time to time to see her reactions to the play and the issues I was presenting. It would create a new starting point in Palestinian theater.

Sanaa put her arm around me.

"Try to relax."

I kissed her on both cheeks and we went to bed. But from that night on, I devoted myself to writing the play.

The following day, I prepared to write. I was interested in something I'd already written down in my notebook:

A bridegroom is preparing for his wedding night, which is arousing fear in his mind. He pays no attention to the fear overwhelming the bride, though in fact, the bride is even more afraid than he is, and her fear only grows when the women start to chant the sad songs that accompany her journey from her father's house to the bridegroom's. In a state of confusion, she enters the room where she will be alone with the bridegroom. In those few crucial minutes, the bridegroom remembers his father's advice—"Cut off the cat's head right away. Otherwise you'll live your whole life in a state of humiliation, and she'll dominate you and get her way with you every time."

Of course, his father's words about cutting off the cat's head are enough for him to understand. He heads for the room where the bride awaits him, and before he goes in, his father beats him on the back with his leather belt, just to make sure that he doesn't slacken and fail to deflower the bride.

He goes into the room and demands that she take off her clothes immediately, not allowing her a moment's delay for any flirtation or foreplay. She undresses, trembling. He takes her roughly, and in a few minutes everything is over.

From that night on, the bride suffers from a pain deep inside her that makes her try to avoid her husband's advances. This aversion persists until he begins to doubt she even likes him. He starts to leave the house for work only after locking the door on her. The windows are not easy to get through, because they are crisscrossed with iron bars. The wife becomes a prisoner in her own house, which she cannot leave. At night, when the husband approaches her bed, she makes a lot of excuses to turn him away, to avoid the pain that follows sex, and which lasts for two or three days. The husband becomes even more exasperated with his wife. His explanations for her behavior, and her reactions to his desire to sleep with her, begin to multiply.

The surprise comes when he searches her handbag and finds in it a front door key that's not his. He can't control his suspicions and there's an altercation. He suspects that she might have had some secret experiences while he was away. She swears solemnly that she is a pure and virtuous *woman, and that she's been doing nothing except sit in the courtyard of the house with some female neighbors to pass the time and gossip. Then, when the hour approaches for him to return to the house, she locks herself in so that he can be confident that the goods have been stored safely in their place. She says that if she hadn't done that, and hadn't acquired an extra key to the house—which one of her brothers worked hard to arrange for her—she would have died of grief in this unbearable domestic prison and would have had to divorce.*

I thought about how I might arrange the text in scenes. I could portray the husband before and after cutting off the cat's head. How tense and nervous he is at first, and how he starts to boast of his masculinity after. Then how suspicious he becomes. I could portray the submissive wife before and after her wedding night, and how the possibilities for pleasure that other married women have told her about fade and turn into an evil, threatening pain and suffering.

Of course, I'll have to put other characters in the story. The father who incited his son to cut off the cat's head; the bride's mother and other members of her family, concerned to see the white handkerchief soaked in the bride's blood; and the bridegroom, who emerges waving it in front of all God's creation, followed by ululations celebrating that the bride had remained a virgin until the moment when the bridegroom penetrated her. I will assign a part to the registrar, who marries the couple. I'll give him an honorable part and not portray him as a greedy and grasping person, waiting impatiently for the food to be served and then greedily gobbling down the rice and meat—which is how Egyptian films portray certain registrars. I won't present him as a character who boasts about what he knows, since in fact he only knows little.

I will surprise the theater troupe with a finished work. I'm sure that the troupe's director and his colleagues will be delighted to discover a new playwright. They'll look at me with admiration, because I will have concealed the play from them until I visit them one evening carrying the black bag in which I keep files for my work in the sharia court. For added effect, I'll make a big deal of opening the bag, and they'll look at me expectantly. They will be astonished to see the polished text of a play, complete with suggestions for casting, décor, lighting, costumes and all the properties needed for an appealing production. As I hand the script to the producer, I'll tell him, *"This story drained the blood from my heart as I wrote it, and I'm certain that audiences will be so affected by it that their hair will stand on end when they see it live on stage."*

I said a lot of things to myself as I tossed and turned on the bed next to Sanaa. The surprising thing is that, while lying awake that night, I wasn't thinking about how to actually write the story or compose scenes in my mind, as writers usually do and as I learned to do later. All my attention was on the moment when I would go to the troupe's office in the evening, open my bag and take out the handwritten text—which was contained in an orange file—give it to the director and wait for his reaction.

As I carefully rehearsed this moment in bed, I became even more emotional and unable to sleep. My bladder felt full, and I kept having to get out of bed and go to the bathroom. Sleep became even more difficult, which made me keep tossing and turning in bed, bumping from time to time against Sanaa's legs, which woke her up and annoyed her. "What's got into you, Muhammad? Why aren't you sleeping?" she asked me, both of us lost in darkness.

I apologized to her and immediately felt her sympathy towards me. I explained that it was the nervousness of an artist on the point of giving birth to an artistic creation. I smiled, without Sanaa noticing. "I'm like a woman getting ready to give birth—my breathing has gotten tense, my muscles taut, and my emotions, fear, and nervousness have all grown stronger, anticipating this child emerging from my womb."

Sanaa said nothing.

My metaphor had flopped, despite the fact that it was apt, as she was sensitive about any mention of pregnancy or childbirth. Still, she understood.

"What you say is correct. I know that from reading about writers' experiences before, during and after writing."

I touched her hair and thanked her for understanding, but she suggested I get some sleep so I'd be able to go to work in the morning.

Sanaa went to sleep, and I tried to but couldn't. I got up quietly from the bed, careful not to disturb her again, and made my way to the guest room. There I tried to sleep on the sofa but couldn't, and remained awake until morning. *This must be the price I have to pay for being a writer. I should bear the burden without complaining or grumbling.*

After I came back from court, Sanaa and I ate lunch. I was worn out. Sanaa noticed but didn't want to make me feel guilty about what had happened the night before. After lunch

I slept for two hours and woke up feeling enthusiastic and determined to work.

I sat at the table where we'd had lunch and said to myself, *After I've finished the play, I'll buy a special table to put in a corner of the sitting-room, where I can write.*

I brought enough paper and pens, opened my notebook with the divorcees' stories in it and started to write. I drew up a plan for the first act. Then I turned to writing the dialogue to begin the scene. I'd write dialogues in Palestinian colloquial Arabic. Since I was familiar with the members of the troupe and the types of characters they played, as well as the character of the troupe's only actress, the dialogue would suit the characters well.

To stir up audience expectations, I'd start with a moving situation, the father advising his son to cut off the cat's head right away. I wrote one sentence, then another. When I thought about the father's third sentence, I found that he had delivered his message in two sentences and had nothing more to add. For his part, the son simply responded with the determination of someone who will shortly be entering battle: "Okay, Father. Okay!"

But I was unable to finish the scene and comforted myself with the thought that even Tawfiq al-Hakim, confronted with a task like this, might not have been able to write it as easily as he hoped. I got up and made for the kitchen, where I heated two cups of coffee, for Sanaa and myself. I told her what I'd gotten done so far. She shook her head as she sipped her coffee and said to keep writing.

I continued my efforts but without success. The lines I wrote didn't hang together, and the scenes lacked the warmth of real experience. I tore up a lot of paper, but Sanaa never stopped encouraging me. She said that tearing up pages was a ritual of gifted writers. So I became more optimistic and began tearing up paper furiously in the hope that the creative devil might take pity on my situation.

Suddenly, I had a brainwave. I recalled a case I hadn't written down in my notebook because the court hadn't considered it. It was the day that war broke out. I recalled the man and the woman who had come for a divorce, and the judge had asked them to come back to court after the war had ended. The war ended, but the man and his wife didn't come back.

I thought about the situation. It was open to several possibilities. Had the man or the woman been killed? Had they perhaps been killed together by a missile that had destroyed their house? Had the man and woman lived through the six days of the war and the humiliation and shame that followed, waiting for what the victors would do to the local people, with the result that harmony returned to the couple under the pressure of unexpected new circumstances? Did the husband take advantage of the opportunity given by the occupiers' announcement that anyone wishing to leave would find buses waiting to transport them free of charge to the bridge? Had he left in one of those buses and headed east, to escape from a wife he didn't want and had no feelings for? Had she left the country with her family, leaving her in a state of limbo without a divorce, which might make her life hell?

I visualized the scenes that might represent this scenario and found them very interesting. I thought, *I will write them for the stage and dazzle the audience.* But when I wrote, only feeble dialogue came out. I explained my situation to Sanaa.

"I'm all worked up and eager to pour out what's inside me. But when I start pouring, what comes out isn't good."

"I don't know the reason for that," she replied, "but creative writing isn't easy."

So I thought about it. *Instead, I will explain my ideas to the troupe and use the improvisation and collective composition method they employ, which makes up for not having playwrights in the country.* This idea made me happy. Perhaps my talent would produce something worthwhile after all, as I worked with the improvised scenes.

But sometimes I just wanted to have a bit of time for contemplation. When the weather was springlike, sweet breezes would blow, white clouds spread across the sky and I wanted nothing more than to sit in the garden in front of my house, away from the eyes of others. Even Sanaa, who knew where I was, would allow me the chance to withdraw like this. She knew I liked to be on my own, observe my surroundings and relieve my nerves of the cares of the world. I would look back and recall experiences in my life, reviewing the years I'd spent as a sharia court employee till now. I had had ambitions.

As a youth, I had wanted to be an actor. But when I found a job in the court, this desire evaporated and an urge to write took its place. Perhaps it was the stories I'd written in my notebook about divorcees, and the way the stories had piled up, that spurred me on to write. For I had all the raw material, which lacked only a good grasp of language.

I was confident that I had a good knowledge of Arabic because of my extensive reading and memorization of the Qur'an and Arabic poetry from various eras. But then I realized that writing requires elements other than just raw material and language. There is an additional quality that has to be present in a person who wants to be a writer: it may be a gift or a particular quality that enters into their material, filling it with vigor and the power to reach readers, without burdening them or lapsing into triviality.

It seemed so easy for actors to perform their parts that I expected I would be able to write dialogue just as easily. But when I started, I found it extremely difficult.

Through experience, it became clear to me that I was not talented and that I would never be able to write a single page with a hint of creativity or flicker of talent. I thought about it and concluded that the reason was my work in the sharia court. How can someone be a writer after spending fifteen years as a court employee, with a job that involves drawing up marriage contracts over and over again in a set style, and issuing inheritance certificates and divorce papers in a prescribed linguistic format? I felt like a prisoner in invisible chains that had turned me into no more than a machine that operated in a routine, mechanical way, without any creativity, which confirmed the menial nature of my place in society.

I got up from where I was sitting in the garden and headed into the house. I found Sanaa in the bedroom, lying on the bed, engrossed in reading a book. When she saw me come in with an emotional expression on my face she stopped reading. "Is something troubling you, Muhammad?" she asked. I didn't reply, but picked up from among the books on the bedside table the notebook in which I'd written stories about the divorcees and headed for the kitchen. Sanaa followed me and stood looking at me from a distance. I lit a match and brought it close to the edge of the notebook until it caught fire. Then I threw it out of the kitchen window.

I looked at Sanaa, who seemed unable to express what she was thinking. Then she asked me, as if she knew what I was thinking, "What else?"

"I'll resign from my job in court."

■

My brother Muhammad al-Kabir didn't approve of my decision. He said, "Maryam and I would be afraid to encourage you to act so hastily."

"I advise you not to quit your job," my mother said, "because you may not find a better job than that one."

Before I made this decision, I had laid the ground for it a year earlier, without planning to do so, when I requested the court to release me from the post of registrar. I could no longer see girls of fourteen and fifteen being married off and taken out of school by their families, on the grounds that at the end of the day a girl's destiny was to be married and to sit at home.

It was during that time that the surprise came. My brother Muhammad al-Kabir was detained again, then removed to Jordan. There he met Fu'ad Nassar, the leader of the party. He had met him for the first time, as I knew, when he came with my brother Youssef first to Ra's al-Naba' and then to the village of 'Arab al-Sawahra because he had been wounded in the shoulder during the 1936 Revolt.

He also met his doctor comrade for whom he had canvassed with Maryam in the 1956 elections, and who had won a seat in Parliament. Muhammad al-Kabir visited him in his clinic in Amman, following which the doctor held a feast for him and a number of other fighters who had been exiled from the occupied territories in his village near the town of Kerak. There my brother Muhammad al-Kabir met a number of Jordanian clansmen, many of whom held views similar to his.

He met Sayil, the husband of our late aunt Ma'zuza, and Fazza', our cousin. My brother sent his news first to his wife Maryam, who had stayed in Jerusalem, and she passed on everything to us whenever she went to visit him. When his time away from the country lasted longer, she joined and stayed with him in Amman.

I said to my father, "The women in our family are treated unjustly." And I gave as an example Fahima, the wife of my brother 'Atwan, who'd left her and traveled far away. She was still waiting for him to come back. I gave him another example: the polygamy in our family. He himself had married six times, and still had four wives—Mathila, Safiyya, Samiha and my mother, Wadha. He had grieved a lot, so he told me, over two wives who had died young—Fatima and Watfa.

He said to me, "I follow God's law, which has allowed us to take two, three or four wives, as seems good to us." And I reminded him of God's words: "And if you fear that you may not be equitable, then one."

He replied, "We, the al-'Abd al-Lat family, have a saying that our men are the servants of our women, to love them and spoil them and not to disobey them in anything. Even the men who are related to us by marriage are like us—they love their wives and spoil them."

And he gave me as examples the Turk Alioğlu, the husband of my aunt Mahyuba, who would carry her on his shoulders all around the house, and the Jordanian Sayil, the husband of my aunt Ma'zuza, who wept in grief for several months when she died.

My mother, who had been listening to the conversation, said, "What you say is true, Mannan, but..."

"But what, Wadha?"

"Tell me how you behave when you are angry, Mannan!"

"Wadha, anger is the exception. We're talking about what normally happens."

My brother Falihan said, "I agree with what my father says. The proof is how well I treat my wife Sheikha and my wife Rasmiyya."

"These rituals don't mean that the women's situations are as they should be," I said.

The scowl on my father's face told me my father didn't share my opinion, but there was no point in provoking him.

■

Some days after this exchange, he alerted me to the need to write the family tree. I don't know how the idea of the family tree sprung up in his head—perhaps from his merchant friends in the city, who boast of their ancestry, as detailed by their family trees that go back hundreds of years. I said I was sorry that they didn't bother to mention the women in the trees. The women seemed to come from a spare rib, as the saying went.

He looked at me, surprised by my comment, and said that the tree was usually put in the room for guests, and it would be inconceivable to put the names of our women in front of their eyes. There might be people among them who lacked any manners or integrity, who would then go around to other guest rooms and spread vile rumors about them.

To provoke him, I suggested that we could make two trees—one for the guest room, with our men's lineages from the most distant ancestor to the youngest grandson, and another for an inside room in the house, with the women's lineages, from the most distant female ancestor to the youngest granddaughter. I reminded him of his grandmother Mahyuba, whose memory was still celebrated by the clan in song. I asked him, "Doesn't this woman deserve to be remembered in a family tree devoted to women?"

He nodded his head. "I testify that she was a woman above all others!" But then he added, "It is the custom, it's tradition, Muhammad, my son. The people of Ra's al-Naba' will humiliate us if they see that we boast of our women. They will say: 'Their women have only gained a position because of the shortage of men.'"

"What do we care about other people?" I said to him.

"Oh, shut up, everyone!" he said. He clearly didn't want to continue the conversation. "Work on the male family tree, and then God grant us happiness!"

"Okay!" I said to him and smiled.

He looked at me calmly, perhaps afraid that I wouldn't do anything for the family, and that all my promises would remain just empty words.

I sat down by myself and reviewed the problems that had beset the clan and the crises they had lived through.

Inside me there stirred the usual conflicting emotions about what to record. I decided, instead of the family tree—which I don't have much faith in—to record the history of the clan (the al-'Abd al-Lat clan). To this day, this is still just an oral history, passed on from one generation to the next, and as generation gives way to generation and interest in the lives of our ancestors fades, it may be lost. I will do something that will please my father.

I turned the idea over in my head and consulted with Sanaa. She was enthusiastic about it, but week after week I put off starting. Then I forgot about it and buried it amid a host of other commitments. But sometimes I found myself dreaming about it.

■

When I saw her in the street, I recognized her immediately and she recognized me.

"I am coming to you," she said.

"What do you want from me?" I said.

"I want you to marry me," she replied.

I was astonished.

"Marry you?"

"Yes, just for one night."

Then she explained to me how her husband had divorced her three times, but when they came to the court to finalize the divorce, the war had put an end to what they had intended to do. She had lived in her family's house all through the war. When it was over, her husband decided to take back his wife, and she wanted to go back to him, being fed up with living in her father's house. But to achieve that, there had to be a new wedding, after she had married another husband and slept with him for a night.

"I am ready to marry you for one night," I told her.

"I will marry you and I will put a sword between us in the bed."

I married her and we withdrew into a bedroom that had been especially prepared for us. She slept on one side of the bed and I slept on the other, and I put the sword between us. But before I could get to sleep, my leg brushed against hers. I don't know whether it was me or her that was the cause of it—most likely, it was her. I saw her grasp the sword and move it away from the bed.

She said, "You are allowed to me and I am allowed to you, and it's only one night."

I said, "It is one night."

She clung to me, and we continued to enjoy the legitimate fruits of love until dawn. In the morning, we emerged from the bridal chamber and found her husband waiting. He seemed to have spent the whole night by the door, hurrying on the sunrise. He looked at me and he looked at the woman he was going to marry that day, and his words spoke volumes. He seemed to have read in our eyes what we had tried to hide. Then he became visibly perturbed and attacked me, sword in hand. I was overcome by fear and awoke in terror as I started to recall the dream and remember the woman whose fate after so many years I did not know.

■

My mother could no longer put off speaking. Almost every day, she would ask how I could accept not having a child. She would start in when she was certain Sanaa wasn't within earshot, because she had noticed how much this subject hurt her. She didn't want to upset Sanaa because I would immediately hear about it.

When she had stopped playing her usual tune, I would beg her not to despair of God's mercy. She would raise her hands to heaven and start reciting spells, beseeching the Lord of Creation to show mercy on Sanaa and myself. She would then heap blame on Sanaa for continuing to refuse to let her perfume her with incense from the edge of her sleeve to ward off jealousy, and refusing to drink water from the "trepidation bowl"—perhaps because she had once been frightened and become sterile, or because she had been touched by someone who lived with us there, which had made her incapable of conceiving.

Things were no longer as before. She started coming to me in the morning to tell me that she had seen the family horse in a dream. She said that she had seen it neighing, whinnying and showing signs of incredible anger, because to be content with a wife without children heralded the breakup of the family, or exposed it to the unknown.

Her face seemed pale as she told me her dream. She constantly repeated the name of God and asked forgiveness and mercy, imploring Him to preserve the family and increase its descendants.

Wadha

My God, how I have suffered on account of my son Muhammad and his wife Sanaa. I said to him, "Your father and I have found you a wonderful bride. Her father is the sheikh of his clan, and her mother has many children."

Muhammad said he was unwilling to marry a second wife and that even if Sanaa agreed to live with a co-wife, he wouldn't agree. He could live his whole life without children.

I thought of going to the fortune-teller in Hebron that I went to when Muhammad was a little child. I thought, *I will go on the pretext of praying in the Sanctuary of Abraham and ask the fortune-teller for two amulets: the first to make Sanaa willing to have a co-wife (I have a favor to ask, by God, I'm afraid she's working a spell on my son Muhammad!), and the second to make my son fall in love with the girl that we told him about.*

The more I thought about it, the more confused I became. My mind was troubled. If Muhammad found out what I had in mind, he would be angry with me. And then again, I didn't know whether that fortune-teller was still alive at all. Years had gone by since I went to him with Muheira.

One afternoon, Muhammad went out of the house and said that he was going to Jerusalem. The weather was on the cold side, and there were clouds in the sky. I watched him as he left and said in an audible voice, "This is an unlucky day." And indeed, after an hour, I was heading for Sanaa's house, next door to my own house, striking my face, tearing my hair out and screaming. The women of the family heard me and came out of their houses anxiously, and Mannan caught me up, worried sick about me.

"What's wrong, Wadha," he asked, "what's happened?"

I screamed in pain and agony. "My son, Muhammad, has died, Mannan, my beloved son has died!"

Sanaa came out of her house with her face screwed up. She stood near me, frightened, not knowing what to say, unable to put a single question to me. Mannan managed to control himself and asked me, "Muhammad al-Asghar has died? Who told you he'd died?"

I didn't reply but continued to shout and soil my face.

"My son, my darling son, Muhammad, has died, he's died!"

I was watching Sanaa and her reactions. I saw her eyes cloud over with emotion. Then she fell on the ground. I raced towards her and repeated the name of God seven times. Then calmly, I said to her, "Muhammad is fine, Sanaa, your husband is fine, my love, don't worry!"

The women of the family were stunned as they followed the expression on my face, which changed from grief to joy.

Mannan was almost angry at me, but the women of the family soothed his anger, remembering what I had said to them before: "I want to expose Sanaa to a great fear, which will drive away the fear she felt before. Then, after this fear, God willing, she will be able to conceive."

When Sanaa found out what I'd done, she concealed her anger and calmly slipped away to her house. I blamed myself because I was exasperated with her and with Muhammad. When Muhammad found out what had happened, he smiled and asked me not to do it again.

I waited, but Sanaa did not become pregnant.

Finally, I said, "Okay, it's better for me that I give my head some rest from this headache!"

13

Muhammad al-Asghar

I was unemployed for an entire year. My father didn't like it. He regarded my job in the sharia court as a privilege that not just anyone could come by. I told him, "Father, I couldn't find myself in that job."

My mother reprimanded me for saying that to my father. He'd make fun of me, mimicking my voice, "I couldn't find myself in that job...I couldn't find myself in that job." He warned me that I would die of hunger as I wandered over the face of the earth, without work.

My brother Falihan criticized me, accusing me of poor judgment and of throwing away a respectable employment opportunity. My brother Salman sent a letter to my parents, expressing regret that I'd left my job and suggesting I travel to Kuwait, in the hope that he could find me a job there.

My father made no comment.

"I won't leave this place," I said, "and will keep on living between Ra's al-Naba' and Jerusalem until I die."

This kind of talk frightened my mother, who said, "May evil stay far away!"

Still, my father shook his head and said nothing.

My brother 'Atwan sent a letter expressing *his* regret that I'd quit my job. He warned me against going to Brazil, because life there wasn't easy. I reassured 'Atwan that I wasn't thinking of traveling, anywhere.

Sanaa stood solidly behind me. "All my salary is here for you," she said. I thanked her from my heart, while the women of the family muttered to one another, "Muhammad al-Asghar has gone soft in the head, for sure, and it's all due to Sanaa's influence."

But they weren't satisfied with that, either. They said she'd let me leave the job so that I would continue to be at her mercy and not divorce her or take a second wife. When I saw them congregating in front of one of their houses in the evening to gossip and pass judgment on other people, I shouted at them, "Have a little shame! Sanaa is a good woman, and she's not conspiring against me."

They were stunned and fell silent, and said nothing more until I'd gone away.

I don't deny that I regretted my attitude towards the women. For at the end of the day, they deserved praise—not blame. Their predisposition for gossiping behind people's backs was just an expression of their wretched circumstances, and the poverty of their lives.

■

I worked with the theater troupe, publicizing their performances, selling tickets and supervising transport of their productions from one town to another, all in return for next to nothing. But I felt content because I was close to a field of work that I loved and could find myself in. I stayed with this for two more years.

One evening, I was coming out of the theater troupe's home in the Sheikh Jarrah Quarter, and Sanaa was with me. The sky was darkened by clouds, and it was threatening to rain. She said she wanted to walk to the square in front of Herod's Gate and from there find a taxi to take us to Ra's al-Naba', and I also wanted to walk. Not long after leaving the building, it began to downpour. Sanaa was pleased because she loved to walk in the rain. So we walked and got drenched, but luckily we'd taken precautions against the winter weather and worn our coats. We decided to run. We ran in the rain as if we were racing, one moment I was in front, the next moment she was. When we ran past the American Colony Hotel, we got tired and went back to walking, though the rain was still pouring down. Sanaa's hair got wet and twisted down her cheeks and neck, but she didn't mind it. We went past the court, now controlled by the occupiers, and past the Hamra Cinema.

There we heard the sound of an explosion and hurried on, hoping to reach Herod's Gate Square before the occupiers' patrols closed off the streets. As we walked on, the rain eased up. We passed the sharia court where I'd worked for years and had almost reached the Post Office building when an armed patrol blocked our path. The soldiers stopped us and stared into our faces. "ID," one of them said.

He flipped through our identity cards, then asked us where we were going.

"Home," I replied.

"Where is home?"

"Ra's al-Naba'."

"Where's Ra's al-Naba'?"

"Not far from here, near Jerusalem."

"What's your name?"

"Muhammad Mannan al-'Abd al-Lat."

"And who's this, with you?"

"My wife."

He looked at her.

"What's your name?"

"Sanaa Youssef."

He looked me in the face.

"Where have you been?"

"At the theater troupe's building."

"What were you doing there?"

"I work there and my wife was with me."

"Did you plant a bomb near the police station?"

"No."

He ordered us to stand a distance from the military vehicle. A number of other pedestrians had also been detained. Sanaa was the only woman among the group, and I was worried that she might be scared. I grasped her hand in mine and looked at her from time to time to reassure her. She seemed a little perturbed, which was understandable, and I was also apprehensive, but both Sanaa and I were ready to put up with anything else these soldiers might do. We were used to it, like the vast majority of our people. A couple of hours later, they detained four or five youths and drove them to jail, then ordered the rest of us—including Sanaa and myself—to go home. So we found a taxi and left.

■

After my experience working with the theater, I went to work as a proofreader with a daily newspaper, called *al-Diya'*. I liked this job, which tested my Arabic. I was praised by the editor, who several times consulted with me on linguistic questions, to which I gave him helpful suggestions, so that my colleagues teasingly gave me the nickname, "Sibawayhi," after the great Persian grammarian of Arabic.

I was particularly interested in the newspaper's culture page. I would study it thoroughly, reading all the essays, stories and poetry. I was preparing for the moment when I would be able to write a literary piece to submit to the page editor for him to publish, and see my name sparkling at the top of it. Then I would hurry home with page in hand, Sanaa would be pleased, and I would be even more pleased. *This is just the beginning,* I thought. My daydreams carried me off far away, and I saw myself as a writer, moving the hearts of admirers, men and women alike.

I stayed up until midnight to write an essay about spring in our country, about flowers blossoming, and the bounty of nature, crops and trees. I thought, *In my writing I'll intertwine the growth and development to which nature aspires with the repression and assassination of ways of life by the occupation.*

After intense effort, I wrote a thousand words. I was anxious to compose the piece so well that only someone thoroughly at home in the Arabic language could emulate it. I wanted to surprise the paper's literary editor with the linguistic talents that God had given me.

When I showed him the text, he read it with me sitting in his office. He told me that my language was sound. I thanked him and continued waiting for him to offer to publish it. Instead, he said, "Our age no longer enjoys the language of dictionaries. A writer needs to approximate the living language of people in what he writes."

I replied, "We have to preserve the purity of our language and to protect it from the language of the masses."

I was surprised to find myself actually saying this, when I had thought of writing a film script in Egyptian colloquial and a play in Palestinian colloquial Arabic, myself! Then, at the next moment, I had persuaded myself that writing a play or a film script was different from writing a literary text.

"We serve our language best if we make it capable of absorbing life and its innovations," he said to me.

"Please tell me, will you publish it?"

"Leave it to me and I'll read it again, and maybe make some revisions to it—with your permission."

I accepted his conditions without arguing, thanked him and left.

The manuscript remained locked up in his desk drawer for three weeks, during which I was on tenterhooks. Finally, the piece appeared, after several sentences had been cut from it. I considered the literary editor's actions to be an arbitrary and patent interference with my ideas, so I wasn't keen to offer him any new writing. In fact, my enthusiasm for writing literary pieces waned.

When I got back home, I showed Sanaa the published piece. She read it and expressed her delight at the excellence of my language and ideas. That somewhat alleviated my feeling of frustration. When I read the text again, though, my worries grew, as I realized that I was confronting a deformed child. I stayed awake, unable to sleep. I saw myself presenting testimony to history amid a crowd of people and placing responsibility for killing my literary talent on the shoulders of the literary editor, who had shown me no pity or mercy. I continued to present my testimony until tiredness caught up with me, and I fell asleep.

While I was sleeping, they came and surrounded me on all sides.

I looked at them carefully and recognized them. They were the men and women whose tragedies I had recorded in my notebook. From the looks in their eyes, it seemed that they were criticizing me because I had set fire to the notebook. I felt an intense sense of regret and wasn't sure how to apologize to them. Should I say I'd been unable to transform their tragedies into literary art with any justice? Before I could reply, the woman who had appeared in a previous dream, for me to marry for one night, reappeared.

"You wronged me in your dream," she told me.

I was surprised.

"How do you know that I dreamed of you?" I asked her.

"I was with you during your dream," she replied.

"How did I wrong you? I married you so as to make it easier for you to go back to your husband."

"In your dream you let slip something that wasn't true."

"How?"

"It was *your* leg that collided with *mine*," she replied.

"Anything else?"

"And it was you that moved the sword away from the bed, not me."

I was ashamed of my dream about my dream.

"You're right, I believe what you say. Does that make you

happy?" I asked her.

"Yes," she replied, "but what's the use?"

She remained silent for a moment, then explained.

"I went back to my husband after that night, but I only stayed with him for three nights. He divorced me because of what happened between you and me that night."

"And how did he know what happened between us?"

"From the looks in our eyes. Also, he was having a dream that looked into our dream."

I struck my hands together.

"There is no security in this world anymore."

Then I looked around, afraid that Sanaa might be having a dream beside me that looked into my own dreams. Suddenly, though, I felt reassured when I dreamt that Sanaa wasn't in bed with me. I was sleeping in the midst of a fertile garden in a faraway place. I looked at the woman.

"What do you want from me, now that your husband has divorced you again?"

"I want you to marry me now," she said.

"That's impossible!" I told her and my body shook as I saw eyes staring at me from every side.

■

For several months, a sense of failure prevented me from writing. Then suddenly, desire reasserted itself. I wrote several pages, which I sent to various newspapers and magazines, except for the paper where I was working—just to spite the literary editor. Unfortunately, none of the pieces I submitted were published in any of the papers or magazines, convincing me that this wasn't my field, either. I considered switching to writing newspaper reports and turning my attention to the 1976 local elections, which the nationalists won in Nablus, Ramallah, Hebron and other Palestinian cities. I wrote two or three pages, before again feeling overcome by frustration, and stopped writing.

Deep inside, I pitied my father, who had placed on me the burden of keeping the family together and following the fates of its sons and daughters. Since I was incapable of accomplishing that with words, I wouldn't be capable of achieving it through action. I apologized to myself for abandoning the task and after a few days told Sanaa of my decision. She sympathized with me, as always, and seemed disturbed by my frustration and the inertia that had overtaken me.

Two days later, Sanaa suggested I rethink my earlier idea, namely to record events in the life of the al-'Abd al-Lat family. If I wanted to expand the subject, I could record events in the life of the entire clan, even though it had split into several different families. But she cautioned me against thinking of publishing these stories. The very idea of publication might lead me to fail, and the conditions of publication—which were sometimes unfair—might hamstring me so that I couldn't write, might even plunge me into a new sense of defeat.

I reconsidered this idea and became enthusiastic about it again, perhaps because I found myself now in a better position than before to start on it, and make something of it. I realized that my desire to set down the events in the life of the family, which had moved from the desert to the hills overlooking Jerusalem and lived through several periods and numerous rulers, had remained dormant deep inside me despite my having abandoned it before.

I decided: *I will record everything I see. I will preserve in my notebooks every word spoken by my mother Wadha, my father Mannan and anyone else in the family. I will give roles to the sons and daughters of my family, and the sons and daughters of the clan, starting from a moment long ago, the killing of grandfather 'Abd Allah, and his mare's grief for him and her departure from the clan's campsite. I will write about the injustice of the Turks in sending our young men to distant battlegrounds, the British Mandate and the arbitrary way in which they treated the country and its people. I will describe how the Mandate soldiers—afraid of mines and ambushes—protected themselves from attacks by the revolutionaries by placing Palestinian prisoners in a vehicle driven in front of the soldiers' own vehicles. I will preserve a record of the massacres of Palestinians the Zionist gangs organized to terrify them into leaving the country; about the loss of the country, the reunification of the two Banks, and about the political repression that was normal before the 1967 defeat. I will tell about the defeat, the ruthlessness of the occupiers, the members of my family, the people of Ra's al-Naba' and the other Palestinians who were martyred, and I will either keep on writing indefinitely, or stop at a decisive moment in time.*

Sanaa thought about my plan and then gave it her blessing, without reservation. I told her, "At the right time, I will reassure my father that I will continue to fulfill his wishes somehow, no matter how many difficulties I may have to overcome."

I thought of telling my brother Falihan that I'd write a *taghriba* for the family like that of the Bani Hilal that he was always quoting. But then I reconsidered, because I would then be exposed to his crimes. I confided to Sanaa, "Discretion is the best way of accomplishing anything, especially when it involves exposing the truth about the policies of rulers—whether the rulers are our own or are interfering strangers."

Sanaa agreed. She said that real writers only revealed their projects after they had completed them, because talking too much—whether at an appropriate time or not—brought bad luck and made it more difficult to accomplish one's objectives.

After a moment, it came to me. "I've got it," I said to Sanaa, and she smiled. "My brother Falihan loves being frank," I said. "I'll just ask him to tell me about everything that concerns him, without explaining. And I'll just listen to my mother, who certainly doesn't need any encouragement to talk!"

14

Wadha

My God, how often have I stood at the doors of prisons and detention camps! When Muhammad al-Kabir was in al-Jafr prison, Mannan would visit him with Maryam. And sometimes, all three of us would visit him. And when Israel imprisoned him, Mannan and Maryam would go to visit him. May God ease his path, Muhammad al-Kabir, he's now living in Amman, and his wife Maryam is living with him there, and she has a permit from the Israeli authorities. When her permit expires, she'll come back home, we'll see her for an hour or two, then she'll go back to her home in Jerusalem, live there for a month or two, visit the Church of the Resurrection and the al-Aqsa Mosque, pick up a sack with some earth from Jerusalem in it, then travel back once again to her husband, give him the sack of earth, and he'll smell it and kiss it and put it close to his heart, poor man!

I tell you, I took it upon myself to visit Adham with Mannan. Adham's mother Watfa died giving birth to his brother, Wattaf, and Adham has no wife or children. Mannan and I used to go from prison to prison in a Red Cross vehicle stuffed full from one end to the other with prisoners' families.

The bus would finish the journey at Ashkelon Prison. My God, how tired and sweaty I used to get! When I saw the barbed wire on the prison walls, my body would shudder. The faces of the policemen there wouldn't smile at a warm loaf!

We would get down from the bus and wait for an hour or two at the door until they allowed us in. They would shout at us as they let us in to a small hall, and the prisoners would stand behind wire mesh. I'd be looking for him in every direction, and Mannan as well, until we spotted Adham. Mannan would stretch his finger through a hole in the mesh, and Adham would stretch out his finger, and that would be the greeting. Then I would do the same as Mannan and ask him, "How are you, Adham?"

"I'm fine," he would reply.

Mannan's tears would pour down his cheeks. I would look into Adham's face and notice how full it was of wrinkles, and his head all white. And after half an hour, the policeman would shout at us.

"Visit over, everyone outside, quickly, quickly!"

We would say goodbye to Adham and leave. I'd already made several visits like this one. How much I have seen and would have liked to have seen!

■

Muhammad al-Asghar

My father was my mother's constant preoccupation, and she didn't hide from me the smallest details of the relationship between them.

That morning, as usual, she made breakfast for both of

them. The siege of Beirut had gone on for two months—the siege that made Sanaa and me cancel our visit there. During the siege, my father grew even more silent. That morning, he and my mother didn't exchange a single word. My mother knew his moods well, and he didn't like a lot of talk in the morning. She knew the sorts of food that he wanted—yogurt with wheat bread, eggs fried in clarified butter, and afterwards, coffee, which he loved to drink.

They sat at the table and ate their food slowly. There was no conversation. "Sure," she said, "but I had things to say, and Mannan certainly had things to say."

My mother felt uneasy because she believed that one could not feel secure with men, especially when there were co-wives lurking not far from the front door—even if she was the youngest of them, and even though her co-wives were quite elderly, as was my father, Mannan.

She snatched a glance at his face from time to time and saw that there were some words inside him getting ready to come out. She ate slowly, and seemed preoccupied, expecting something or other.

Calmly, as he drank his coffee (though with a certain hidden tension in his voice), he said, "I want to sleep with my other wives, because if God, may He be praised and exalted, takes me to Himself, I want to face him with my conscience at peace. Did you hear what I said, Wadha?"

"I heard you."

He had noticed that my mother didn't feel comfortable with what he had said, even though she had formally agreed to it. But he paid no attention to her discomfort, and started to put his wishes into practice. Mathila accepted him, because her relations with him had improved since the night when his mother, Sabha, had died. Samiha did not accept him. She told the women of the family that she found it odd that he should come back to her after years of shunning her. She still remembered how he had come back to her after her son Youssef's martyrdom and had carried on returning to her bed for two or three years, then abandoned her. She said she didn't want to be his servant again. She suggested to him that he stay with Wadha, who had squeezed him dry and now wanted to throw him away like a piece of dried-up peel. When my mother heard this, she protested. "I squeezed him dry? I want to throw him out? God strike her blind!'

My father wasn't expecting this sort of attitude from Samiha. He thought she would welcome him and was furious. He ranted and raved, with threats and curses. "I come to you and you reject me, Samiha?" he asked, reproachfully. Then he threatened to complain about her to her son Salman, who worked in Kuwait. Samiha remained silent, as though taking pleasure in the attitude she'd adopted. "Remember that I am your husband, good woman!" he told her, trying to act reasonable and wise.

Samiha said a lot of things to the women of the family. She said he had left her, but no comment was to be heard from her on his final words. My mother said that by adopting this attitude, Samiha had tried to take revenge on my father. She said that my father had begun to sense the end and wanted to win Samiha over, just as he had won Mathila over previously.

My mother reluctantly continued to put up with his going to his other wives, but at the same time expressed some annoyance, in the hope that he might abandon his endeavor. The next night, she said she'd seen him slip away from her and go to Safiyya, his fourth wife in order of precedence.

"He hadn't gone to sleep when I got up to check that the door was closed. I got up because I was always on edge, uncertain whether he had locked the door before he went to sleep."

This wasn't the only time that my mother had gotten up and gone over to the door. She was certain he hadn't gone to bed. He didn't sleep more than three hours. "I know his habits," she said. "He tosses and turns in bed and thinks about everything—about the siege of Beirut, which worries him, and about his grandson, Omar, who is there. Sometimes I go over to him and touch his worried brow," she went on.

> I feel the skin on his head, which has almost lost its hair. He doesn't show any enthusiasm for this sort of teasing, but he doesn't complain either, and I don't go too far. I want to make him feel that I am near him, and I cannot leave him to spend what remains of his life alone. I notice that he doesn't sleep at night, so I ask him if something is keeping him awake. He scratches his head as usual, but says nothing. That night, he got out of bed and put on his abaya, thinking that I was fast asleep. Then he went to Samiha's room, as if he had learned nothing from being turned away before. He stood near the door and stretched his hand out, then hesitated and didn't knock. He headed for Safiyya's room. I know her, she sleeps soundly and never wakes until after sunrise. He went up to the door and knocked on it, cleared his throat and waited, but Safiyya did not open the door to him. He went out to the

courtyard and stood near the mulberry tree. He looked at the houses, floating in the darkness. He looked to the east, towards the desert he had come from years ago. He seemed to be contemplating his long journey through life.

I scolded him because he had gone out of the house and left the door open. "Mannan," I said, "you might have let thieves into the house by doing that. Maybe the army would have walked past the house and started to ask us why you're leaving your house door open at this time?"

"No, don't be afraid, Wadha, trust in God, let's go in and sleep!"

The following morning, at the usual gathering of the women of the family, Safiyya revealed the secret without any beating about the bush. She said she had heard him knocking on the door and had decided not to respond. She said she had entertained him some weeks previously in her bed and had regretted it; he had been panting so hard with her in his arms that she thought he was about to breathe his last and die.

■

I found myself being drawn into the details of my parents' lives. Sometimes I was a willing accomplice, drawn on by curiosity—though at other times I was less willing because I felt embarrassed.

She told me she didn't like him leaving his bed for the courtyard of the house. He went out believing she was asleep. That meant he didn't want her to know why he was going out during the night. If he had wanted her to know, he would have told her before she went to sleep. She didn't believe that he went out for a breath of fresh air or to calm down a little, before coming back to his bed to sleep. She thought it unlikely because he had never left the house before at this sort of hour. But how was she to know? Perhaps he had often gone out without her waking up. Perhaps he had often spent time outside the house, then returned to his bed while she was sound asleep. Her suspicions grew, and she became more agitated. How many times had he left the house while she was asleep?

She recalled how open he had been with her about his other wives, and she recalled that she had agreed to what he was proposing, although she hadn't been able to accept it, and he had noticed how disturbed she had been when he started to put his ideas into practice. It seems that for this reason he had started to slip out of bed beside her in order to fulfill his desires in secret, so that she wouldn't startle him, or he her, for at the end of the day she was his youngest wife, and he couldn't do without her or bear to anger her in any way. The whole family knew the extent of her influence on him. One word from her against any of the women or men of the family would make him quiver with anger, and he would quickly pick a fight with the woman or man in question in order to please her.

My mother realized that he engaged in certain activities at night behind her back. She recalled their temporary residence in Hebron those years ago. She recalled the young widow with whom he almost became involved in an intimate relationship, had she not become aware of it from the first moment. She revealed her secret to me in a moment of emotion, and said that after leaving Jericho and returning to Ra's al-Naba', he had tried to go back there more than once. She said she had stopped him from going and wondered, "How would I know if he was going to Jericho behind my back without my knowledge, just as he is doing now?"

My mother became prey to the rumors she had suffered from ever since my father returned to Samiha, Youssef's mother—the co-wife who had suffered the martyrdom of her son. She became the wife who was closer to him than any of the others. "At first, I left him to comfort her," she said. "Her son had been martyred, God help her! He started to stay at her house every night, and she grew more youthful again; none of the other women were like her! He did leave her bed eventually," she said. "But he stayed with her a long time. God is my helper, it's as if he'd married her all over again, as if she was a bride!"

My mother felt more injured than the other wives, because she was the most youthful of them. Samiha bint Hussein al-Shuweifat, Youssef's mother, became the most dangerous of her co-wives, and she suffered bitterly. But this infatuation with Samiha only lasted for seven months, no more. Then my father lost interest in her, and started going back to her once a week, then once every two weeks, then once a month. In the third year, he stopped visiting her altogether. My mother said, "I pray in one room and Mannan prays in another."

I pray, and am afraid whenever evening comes. The darkness still frightens me and makes my body shudder. Ever since those far-off days in the desert, I've been afraid of the dark. From the day we traveled to Ra's al-Naba', I've been afraid of it. It's true, we've got electricity in the house, but there's darkness everywhere outside the house. And when I hear news of the siege, I am even more afraid, and recall that we are living under occupation, under siege. "An army patrol might pass by the house," I said, "and something unpleasant might happen to us. Let's shut the door at prayer time, Mannan," but he refused. "Night hasn't come yet, Wadha," he said to me, "and a guest might arrive."

I know that he likes guests to come. That's something he inherited from the desert, and it came with him to Ra's al-Naba'. But I've had to bear the whole burden. I've stayed up for long nights to serve guests until they've grown tired and gone to bed.

■

Rio de Janeiro
August 15, 1982

Father, I'm so happy that my son Mannan has finished school and found a job as a taxi driver with a monthly salary, so that he has money to spend on himself and his mother. I will continue to send as much money as possible to him and Fahima, in the hope that he will save enough to help him find a nice girl to marry, who will help him to cope with the hardships of life, and stay with him in sickness and in health.

If you ask about us, Father, we are well, thanks be to God. Our son, Simon Bolivar, sends you a thousand greetings. He finished school this summer, and now we will enroll him in university to study engineering at the

University of Rio de Janeiro. And because he is first-rate at his studies, we expect that he will get a scholarship, which will spare us having to pay his fees.

I understand from my brother Salman that he was with you, with his wife and three children, and that they came across the bridge with a permit from the occupation authorities last summer. He told me he was very happy to see you, but that the general situation in the country was extremely bad.

I send you from here a thousand greetings to anyone who asks about us.

Your loving son,
'Atwan Mannan

15

Muhammad al-Asghar

As the siege of Beirut dragged on, Sanaa's mental state deteriorated. She became overcome by the feeling that she herself was under siege. Whenever she saw my mother, she'd become agitated, unable to remain in her presence, and would disappear into her bedroom. My mother didn't intend her any harm. She had put up with the situation that we'd ended up in and had surrendered herself to God. But a passing glance at Sanaa's belly would arouse associations lurking in her mind, and memory. Then silence would prevail for some moments, until we could calm the atmosphere with words and smiles.

I suggested to Sanaa that we go to Haifa. We would sleep in a hotel and swim in the sea. But she wasn't enthusiastic. She said that going to Haifa would make her suffering worse. It would remind her of a past filled with oppression, killing and blood, and of a present that was even more unbearable. She would like to take a trip that didn't stir up such painful memories.

After the 1967 defeat, we had made a trip to the seaside to get to know the Palestinian cities that we'd never seen before. Four of us went—my brother Muhammad al-Kabir, his wife Maryam, Sanaa and myself. We had observed how, after the defeat, the whole of Palestine had fallen under occupation so that Palestinians were now more open to one another. We met with a number of Resistance poets and writers in the areas that had been occupied in 1948. We visited the Gaza Strip and made the acquaintance of some leading literary and political figures there.

We had visited Jaffa, Haifa, Acre and Nazareth. We were shaken that our cities were no longer our own. My brother Muhammad al-Kabir took us to the al-'Ajami Quarter and recalled his days in Jaffa more than thirty years before. At that time, he was a young man who couldn't bear to stay with his clan, living in the desert, so he headed west and settled in Jaffa to work in a restaurant. We set out to visit the restaurant where he had been employed. When we found the place, the Jewish proprietor told us that the conflagration against the Jews, kindled by Hitler, had killed his mother and father, so he had emigrated to Palestine and settled here. He told us that he had the right to do as he liked with his restaurant, which before him had belonged to a Palestinian in Jaffa. We learned from a resident who had remained in the city that the Palestinian proprietor had left the restaurant as the city was falling and had fled abroad with his family.

Seeing again the old, tumbledown houses, I was reminded of a trip to Jaffa with my father and mother when I was a young child. I said to my brother Muhammad al-Kabir, "It looks to me as though Jaffa is ashamed of what has happened to it, don't you think?" My brother gazed at the houses and city. "It could be. But perhaps the shame comes from within ourselves," he replied, shaking his head.

"The houses feel shame when they see their owners coming and are unable to receive them," said Maryam.

"I can clearly see shame in Jerusalem, and I am myself ashamed when I see it," Sanaa admitted.

Then we left.

We had had the same experience when Sanaa and I went to visit my sister Falha at Eid. That was a year before the June defeat. I had visited her several times. The camp was soaking in mud after heavy rain. In every direction I looked, I could see houses crouching quietly. Whenever I visited a Palestinian town or village, I had the same feeling, of shame dominating everything—houses, towns, and villages, and a sense of inferiority grew inside me.

Some weeks after the defeat, we went with our sister Falha and her husband Nu'man to visit his village—Wasmiyya. Rasmiyya and her father, 'Abd al-Fattah, were with us as well (Falihan didn't go). The village was gone, though we found some fig trees still there. The houses had been wiped out of existence and the place turned into an enormous farm. How humiliated and disgusted we felt.

We passed through Palestinian villages that still had their inhabitants in them, even though the occupiers confiscated most of the farmland. We cheered up a little when we found some remnants of our people living in Nazareth, and in some quarters in Acre, Haifa and Jaffa. And whenever we visited the western part of Jerusalem, we felt ourselves being murdered by grief.

So I suggested to Sanaa that we travel to 'Aqaba. On our way, we could visit Petra and explore the Nabataean ruins there, then spend a few days in the Gulf of 'Aqaba, looking at the water. We recalled the warmth of our relationship and our determination to stay together, despite the challenges that had confronted us over the years. When we returned from 'Aqaba to Amman, we could visit my brother Muhammad al-Kabir, who had been in exile for eight years, and his wife Maryam. We could take a diversion to Madaba to visit Sayil, the husband of my late aunt Ma'zuza, check on my cousin Fazza', and stay two or three days there before returning to Jerusalem.

Sanaa wasn't enthusiastic about my idea. She said she preferred to forget her relations and in-laws, and everyone connected with the al-'Abd al-Lat family, even if it was just for a week. I respected her point of view and understood the causes of her anguish. So I suggested to her, "We could travel to Spain. And don't tell me that you don't want to be reminded of our defeat there, centuries ago. Our memories have kept only a few remnants of that defeat."

She laughed, perhaps so that I wouldn't accuse her of complicating things, and agreed to go to Spain.

■

We disembarked at Malaga Airport and were taken by taxi to a hotel in the town center, where we showered and then ventured out. We wandered enjoyably around the streets, noticing the contentment etched on people's faces. We recalled our sufferings in our own occupied country. While walking around, we saw a woman carrying a child in her belly, and she was walking proudly. Sanaa gazed at the woman, then looked away at the trees lining the sidewalk.

We ate supper in a restaurant that served grilled fish, and we gossiped about all sorts of things. Then I took some pictures of Sanaa sitting at the restaurant table, as well as some of her outside on the sidewalk. We asked a passerby to take a picture of us standing together by a tree. I embraced Sanaa, and we smiled into the camera. The passerby took not just one but two pictures of us, and we thanked him!

In the morning, we ate breakfast in the hotel restaurant, then went up to our room and got ready to go to the beach. As Sanaa took off her dress and underclothes, her body looked youthful. She put on the swimsuit I'd bought for her at a shop in Salah al-Din Street in Jerusalem. At her request, I had also bought her some modest pants with bra attached, which covered most of her body. I was surprised that she had thought of wearing a swimsuit, which she hadn't even considered doing when she was twenty-five—and now she was forty-five. Did getting older have something to do with it, a desire to assert that her body was still youthful? Was it a secret wish from years gone by that had persisted, and moved her to put it on now? Had the fact that she was abroad tempted her to wear it? But in the past we had traveled to Turkey. We had gone down to the sea, and she'd only done what she always had before—lifted her dress above her knees and stepped into the water.

Was it a reaction to the silent and not-so-silent struggle between her and my mother? Sanaa wanted to live her own life, without attaching too much importance to the nods and winks, the concealed disparagements, the talk of the women of the family directed at her from time to time, as if the women were the reserve troops for my mother's struggle with her. Sanaa's feelings would be unsettled and hurt; then she would rise above her wounds and continue with her life, though when she became too agitated, she would whisper in my ear when we were in bed, "Come on, let's separate, you'll marry a woman who will give you ten children, as your mother would like, and I'll live alone for the rest of my life after trying two husbands."

"Please stop that sort of talk," I'd say to her. Then I would kiss her on the cheek and she would calm down, and we would go to sleep.

I didn't ask her about it, so as not to embarrass her. When she looked at herself in the mirror, she seemed happy. I watched her and felt how proud I was of her. She put on the dress over the swimsuit, and we went out to the beach.

Holding hands, she was shy walking barefoot, with a lot of men and women lying on the sand around her. She was surprised to see women in revealing swimsuits racing along the shore, then throwing themselves into the water, while the men around them joked with them and sprayed water over themselves.

We went into the water. She stood still in the waves, which barely covered her knees. Cautiously, she waded into deeper water, and I reassured her. She lay on her back in the water, and I held her in my arms. I encouraged her to move her arms and legs, and she did. But after a time she became frightened and took in some water. So we went back to the shore. As we lay on the sand, she stopped feeling embarrassed at wearing her swim-suit in public. We spent a refreshing time together on the beach.

During the following days, we divided our time between the sea and visits to archaeological sites in Malaga. We visited the city's historic citadel, and the house where the painter Pablo Picasso was born, which held some of his personal possessions and a number of his paintings. For ten days in Spain, we shook off our preoccupations and felt relaxed and bought souvenirs. Then we went back to Jerusalem where, after the June defeat, the occupiers had extended the city limits, and Ra's al-Naba' had become a suburb of Jerusalem. Sanaa was happy, and had gotten a bit of a suntan. And I was happy, because I had brought some happiness to her heart. But our happiness lasted only a short time.

■

"Mannan's not his usual self," my mother said to me. "He's changed, maybe because of the troubles. Who would have thought that Palestine would be lost and its people would become refugees? It's so dreadful. Mannan had such high hopes when the 1967 war happened!"

"When the 1973 Ramadan War broke out," my mother continued, "Mannan would watch television and call out, 'We've won!' But our situation remained just as it was. Mannan would cry, 'God have mercy on you, Gamal Abdul Nasser, you left us too early!' What can I say? Your father's worries increased. His mind was preoccupied with the children of the family, who had been dispersed all over the place."

Several times I asked my mother to encourage him to take a rest from thinking about the family and clan, and about our present situation. "I gave him the advice, Muhammad, but your father's head is like granite, he doesn't listen or take advice."

"Be fair to him, Mother. Father gives and takes, he listens to the person talking to him and thinks about what he's heard."

"That was a long time ago, son. Now your father is stubborn, and I don't know what to do with him. But I'm hiding my heartaches and only telling them to you, Muhammad."

I felt for my mother's suffering and hoped she'd be able to put up with my father, because he really wasn't like he used to be. Age had its own rules.

■

Rio de Janeiro
September, 15 1982

Father, Giselle and I are concerned about you. When we received your last letter, we reckoned that your health could not be good. We thought of getting on the first plane back home. Then we recalled that we had sworn never to enter Jerusalem while it was under occupation, so forgive us, Father. Your understanding is sufficient. I'm sure that you are a strong man, as I know you are, and that you'll be able to get over your illness and continue to enjoy health and happiness until Jerusalem is liberated and we can come to visit you, and you us.

A thousand greetings from Giselle and me, and farewell!

Your loving son,
'Atwan Mannan

My brother Falihan responded that 'Atwan seemed like "someone ploughing the sea."

If I were living abroad, I wouldn't have waited for a single moment, wouldn't have hesitated to come home to reassure myself about my father's health. It's his duty to come to see his wife Fahima, and his son Mannan. It's his duty to come home, whether our country is under occupation or has been liberated. This is our country and it's our right to go back to it, without anything getting in the way of our return. 'Atwan now has a Brazilian passport and can come back.

Falihan suggested I allow him to reply to 'Atwan's letter. "I'll say to him, 'Please get Sitt Giselle's permission to let you visit your father and your mother, who are longing for you, as well as your wife Fahima, who has been patient for many years.'"

■

My mother was angry with Sanaa when she heard about our time at the beach.

My God, I have seen so many terrible things! How angry I was when I saw my daughter-in-law coming back from her trip and found out what had happened. Lord, I didn't see anything at all, but she herself told the women about everything she'd done there. She told it as though she was trying to make me angry, or show off how beautiful she was. She took herself into the water and the sea embraced her and submerged her shamelessly. And I, Wadha daughter of 'Abd al-Hadi, know that the sea is a male that leads women astray. She said she wore a swimming outfit that covered only half her body. And she wasn't satisfied with just talking about it. She lifted up her dress up and let the women see how her thighs had gotten sunburned from sitting on the beach under the summer sun for such a long time—in front of strangers.

I, Wadha, daughter of 'Abd al-Hadi, say this, may God help me! Sanaa did what she did and lifted her dress in front of the women to prove to them that she is still a young woman, and that her body wouldn't have stayed so youthful if she had bothered to get pregnant and have children.

Out of the blue came a letter from 'Atwan.

Rio de Janeiro
October 17, 1982

A fair greeting, gentler than a breeze, which comes and goes from a wounded heart to the beloved of spirit, my dear Father, Mannan Muhammad al-'Abd al-Lat. After kissing your pure hands, Father, I will reassure you about my circumstances. I am well and do not lack anything except to see you all. I give you and Mother a thousand greetings. I hope that you will get better soon. Giselle also sends you a thousand greetings.

The news is that Simon has gone to live with his girlfriend in a suburb near our house (life here is chaotic, Father, I will not hide anything from you). And because Giselle and I felt lonely after Simon had moved out, we decided to adopt a little girl from the orphanage. We brought her home with us and her name is Janet, but she has another name that I gave her—Mathila, hoping that my mother will like that and consider it a token of love and devotion.

Honestly, Father, I was really hurt by the harsh words that my brother Falihan directed towards me in the letter that I received from you some days ago. Thank God that Falihan was only speaking for himself and not for you, Father. I know that you are honest in what you say, and that you cannot make me angry while I am in a foreign country. My brother Falihan accuses me of being remiss, when I dream night and day of our country. By the way, since Beirut fell under siege, we took the initiative to form a pressure group to break the siege. When the Sabra and Shatila massacre happened, our emotions were aroused, as were the feelings of the Brazilians, who expressed their solidarity with the betrayed camps and with the Palestinians, as well as with the Lebanese whose country had been subjected to invasion, and whose beautiful capital had been besieged.

But to return to the subject, Father. Allow me to address some words to my brother Falihan and inform him that I have more concern than he does for the family, and its cohesion and harmony. Here in exile, I represent the conscience of the family and promote it. I am confident that when the people of Ra's al-Naba' count the successful men of the village, they will put my name at the top of the list, and when they count the respectable men of the village, who do not deal in dirty money, they will put my name at the top. Father, for the first time I will tell you a secret. Among the reasons I quit the job in my brother Falihan's bar, it wasn't just the low wage I received but also because I was dealing in my brother's dirty money, and because the Lord of Creation will hold me to account for my silence and consent. I couldn't continue working with him, and that was the end of it.

I tell you frankly, Father, my financial circumstances don't allow me to squander unlimited amounts of money. Our circumstances here are hard. If I was able to save up the price of a ticket to Palestine and to make the financial commitments necessary for me to visit you, I wouldn't hesitate to come.

Forgive me, Father, I wish you good health and a long life, and hope that my circumstances will improve at a later date, so that we can meet on the soil of the homeland. I hope that my brother Falihan won't be angry with my frankness, for I am first and foremost his brother, who wishes him health, happiness and a good reputation among people.

A thousand greetings from me to my brother, Muhammad al-Asghar.

Greetings, and farewell.

Your loving son,
'Atwan Mannan al-'Abd al-Lat

■

My father paid no attention to my brother's letter. He was no longer capable of sitting still. He would sit in his guest room for a few minutes and then leave, taking no notice of the fact that he had guests. He would leave them and go outside, while one of my brothers or another member of the clan would apologize to the guests and sit with them, making polite conversation until they had eaten their lunch and drunk their coffee, before leaving happily.

He began to express a wish to visit the desert again. We

suggested that we should go with him, but he would not agree.

He went on foot. We were amazed at how well he could walk, despite his advanced age. He said, "If I had a horse, I would ride it and go into the desert every week." But he had given up breeding horses years ago, so he started going to the desert on foot. He would sit at the side of the road to rest, then continue walking without hurrying too much. He visited the districts of Sararat, Jinjis, Dumnat Hilal and Umm Rayyan. He would gaze at Mount Mintar from a distance but not dare to go there for fear that the effort of climbing the mountain would be too great. He visited the tombs of his father and his grandfather and grandmother, as well as other deceased relatives from the clan, but he didn't dare go near the Israeli settlements that had been built there. Then he would come back from the desert, unable to resettle himself.

He would also go to Jerusalem on foot, taking the same route he'd taken before the 1948 disaster. He would cross the street that passed in front of the High Commissioner's residence, enter the suburb of Tell Buyut, walk by the Sultan's Pool and Herod's Gate, then go through the large gate and walk through the markets that would lead him to al-Aqsa Mosque. There he would wander around the courtyards and perform the noon and afternoon prayers. He would leave the mosque, irritated by the sight of the military patrols stationed at the crossroads by the markets or wandering amid the people, weapons in their hands. He would sigh in sadness and anger, and recall his martyred son Wattaf and his martyred wife Mirwada. He would recall his martyred son Youssef and thousands of other martyrs, and the tears would fall from his eyes. Then he would sadly return to Ra's al-Naba'.

He began to suffer moments of absentmindedness, when he would walk with bowed head, talking aloud to himself. Then he wouldn't hesitate to ask a question he'd repeated a lot in recent days: "Was I right to leave the desert?"

We would reassure him and tell him, "Of course you were right. Look around you at the houses in Ra's al-Naba' and at its sons and daughters, and you'll see that you were right."

He would calm down a bit, but become agitated again. He would get up and leave the guest room and walk between the houses. He would look at the village, which was full of children, full of his grandsons and granddaughters. Then he would go back to the guest room and sit among us, gazing at us and saying, "I shouldn't have left my father's and grandfather's tomb in the desert. I should have stayed there, acquiring horses and cattle."

We would try to calm him and put his mind at ease. "We haven't forgotten, and won't forget, our ancestors. We will continue to remember and recall them. But we have our life now, which we think is better than our grandfathers' life in the desert. And you can still go there from time to time."

He would shake his head as if unconvinced by what we were saying, then fall silent, no longer wanting to speak. After a time, he would leave the guest room and walk aimlessly down the lanes of Ra's al-Naba'. We would follow him and persuade him to come back home. Without arguing, he'd give in to our wishes and come back.

■

As Father's condition worsened, my mother dumped her sorrows on my shoulders. He stayed in bed for seven days. Each night, we gathered around his bed, comforting and encouraging him, telling him that he was well and that he only had to bear the pain. He would open and close his eyes, moan and ask, "How can I get better?" Then, after a moment's silence, he would say, "I see them every night."

"Who?" we would ask.

"My father Muhammad, my grandfather 'Abd Allah, my grandmother Mahyuba, and my mother Sabha. I see them, I sit with them, and I drink coffee with them. They drink coffee with me. They get up and insist that I go with them. They grasp my hand, while I insist that they stay in my guest room. They insist on going because they can't stay. Then I wake and tell them, 'It's my turn to go.'"

My mother's spirits plummeted. She turned her head so that he could not see her and wiped away her tears. He looked at our faces. His gaze settled on mine, thinking of something to say to me, but hesitating. Overcoming his reluctance, he said, "The al-'Abd al-Lat family is a trust around your neck, Muhammad." Then after a moment, he added, "And do not forget the clan."

As I clung to his hand, I nodded my head to acknowledge his words. "Don't worry, Father, don't worry." But at the bottom of my heart, I ask myself, *What can I do for the family and the clan?*

I believe that deep within, he was in despair, too, and was trying to hold on to the remnants of a hope that was still there, hidden inside him and which he somehow had to make public. His eyes fell on Sanaa's face. He looked at her carefully. He must have felt regret because she hadn't produced a single child to enrich the life of the family. He didn't want to anger her, so he smiled at her despite his pain and she clutched his hand, tears in her eyes.

Despite his illness, he knew that the siege of Beirut had ended, leaving many dead, and that the Resistance had left Lebanon. He knew that his grandson Omar, the son of my brother, Muhammad al-Kabir, had left for Tunis with the Resistance, with his Lebanese wife and three children. He didn't know if this war would be followed by other wars or not. He started to hum gently a few lines he could recall from the *taghriba*.

The girl of the quarter, Umm Muhammad, says,
tears flowing down her cheeks,
I wish I had died a year ago
and not seen the Amir Abu Zayd killed

My mother gestured to him to stop humming, as if she could sense an evil omen in the grief-stricken tone in his voice.

■

Over the coming days, my mother continued to administer medicines to my father, but to no avail. We whispered to each other, "There's nothing can be done."

My mother made him smell the edge of her *thob* for fear that he might have been exposed to enviers and to sow jealousy in the heart of her co-wives who were gathered there around him. She remained the pampered one who had enjoyed his love and sympathy over the long years. That wasn't the whole story, but my mother, with her extreme sense of discretion, had left no room for the women of the family to know a single one of the secrets she enjoyed with him.

He could not bear the smell of incense, and a frown came

over his face that made my mother smile despite herself. He paid no attention to her smile, which had previously captivated him. His health worsened and none of her remedies did any good. We took him to the hospital, then brought him back home. We were expecting him to go at any moment.

He saw Falihan in his wheelchair, but his eyes settled on him for only a few moments. He looked at Rasmiyya and seemed happy with her. My mother asked him, "How do you feel, Mannan?"

He didn't reply. He looked at Mathila, Safiyya, and Samiha. What could he say to them now? He said nothing for a long time, as if recalling his days with them. My mother broke his chain of thought, because it seemed she didn't want his gaze to linger on them longer than necessary. "May God make your days fruitful, Mannan!" she said.

He looked at my mother, watching her with wandering eyes. She came nearer to him and kissed his brow. *Even at these critical moments, she wants to have a monopoly over him and exclude his other wives,* I thought. His other sons and daughters, grandsons and granddaughters, brothers and sisters hovered around him. He had more than two hundred descendants. And now he was on the point of death. I was convinced that his life hadn't been in vain. He had lived a life brimming with experiences, filled with joys and sorrows, sometimes with riches, at other times with very little money. When my sister Falha came up to him, he looked in her eyes, and she kissed his brow and wept.

■

Since his condition had gone downhill, the women of the family had become accustomed to gathering in the courtyard near to the room where he slept, staying there until midnight, and opening all the files, so to speak. There was no one in the family or the clan, so my mother told me, who hadn't been the subject of a good word from them, if he was deserving of praise, or an ugly word if he deserved censure. There wasn't a woman in the family or clan—except for those who were gathered in the courtyard—who hadn't at some time been praised, accused or made the subject of a sarcastic remark or piece of gossip that hadn't circulated before.

My mother said she felt afraid when she saw them in the courtyard, all together, nothing moving except their tongues, as they rehearsed both the fertile and the dry parts of the clan's long history, sifting through the details, and putting the good on one side and the bad on the other. There was not one family secret left that hadn't been uncovered. Meanwhile, my mother was thinking about the need to spray the courtyard with water to calm the anger of the jinn who lived there with us, and who would not be pleased by the women's gathering.

If my mother hadn't been interested in listening to every detail, large or small, she wouldn't have sat with them, for fear of the harm that might overtake her from the jinn. But her concern for the family and her interest in all its affairs drove her to sit with them.

Rasmiyya, so my mother said, had an unusual attitude that marked her off from the others. When she was in her own house, built on our land to the north of Jerusalem near the al-'Awda camp, she didn't take part in gossip, and when she was in her house in Ra's al-Naba' near Jerusalem, she stayed in her house and took no notice of the women's get-togethers, though she didn't escape their tongues.

Other women also did not escape their tongues. Claudia, who had quarreled with Adham in Amsterdam, received her share of their accusations, despite the fact that they had never met her. "A slut, God curse her!" they whispered to each other. And as proof of that, they pointed to the fact that Adham had lived with her without marrying her. Najma and her daughter Nawal were also within firing range, and were not safe from their nods and winks, because they had settled in the city. Giselle, whom they accused of preventing 'Atwan from visiting the homeland to say farewell to his father, also received her share of their blame and criticism. They said she walked in the street in short skirts that showed her thighs, and a blouse that half-revealed her breasts.

When Sanaa was sitting with them, her case remained closed, only to be opened after she had left. But she generally didn't sit long in the courtyard. After she had left, they resumed their gossip, oblivious to the presence of my mother among them, perhaps because they anticipated that she would not get in their way. My mother didn't interfere with their right to speak, because, so she told me, she loved to listen to their gossip, even if the gossip was pure fantasy and rumor.

After this, she would proceed to sift the wheat from the chaff and choose which stories she wanted to repeat and pass on in their evening get-togethers.

The women of the family and some women of the clan continued to gather in the courtyard every evening.

■

It was now six days and nights since my father's health had started to decline, but he was still alive. On the morning of the seventh day, my mother said that an owl with a high-pitched call had been screeching throughout the previous night. She had thought it an ill omen, got out of bed and gathered her courage to leave the house. She said, "I screamed at it and drove it out, shouting, 'Go away you wretch, go, take your mischief away!'"

She said the owl returned a little later and continued its screeching.

That night, my mother drove it away seven times and realized that my father would die. She said she slept only at dawn, and she wished she hadn't slept because in a dream she saw the family mare running around the clan houses, neighing and frothing at the mouth. As it approached our house, it stumbled on some ropes set up between the tents, which the jinn who lived with us there had set up, and its body dropped to the ground. It continued neighing as it tried to get up, but without success. She said, "I woke up, asked God for refuge from the accursed Satan and looked at Mannan. He was breathing with difficulty and raving. I said, 'God ease for you your death throes, Mannan.'"

I tried to calm my mother's agitated state. I was near my father's bed, she and I taking turns to moisten his tongue and lips with a little water. I looked at the expression on his pallid face and recalled him when he was in his prime—a man with strong features who was feared by other men. I could see that in spite of his shrinking public role in his last years, he and his generation had somehow played their part.

My father had lived under Turkish rule in his youth, and they could have led him off to one of their wars to be killed while still in the prime of life. He had lived in the shadow of the British Mandate, and the British installed him as head of the clan after my grandfather Muhammad was no longer able to perform the duties he had inherited from his father 'Abd Allah. My father had also taken part in the 1936 revolt with my uncle 'Abbas, my brother Youssef and a number of fellow clansmen. He lived through all the defeats from the 1948 disaster to the 1967 defeat, and experienced sorrow, pain and humiliation like hundreds of thousands of his people. He loved his country, even though he was sometimes inclined to withdraw or compromise for fear of the tyranny of the rulers or the cruelty of the occupiers. He didn't steal or cheat or deal in dirty money, but he sympathized with my brother Falihan over his money laundering.

He married six times. He let me in on one of his secrets, saying that when he and my mother took me to Jericho when I was a small child, a dark-skinned widow—one of our neighbors—caught his attention. He liked her and thought of asking her family for her hand. But in this case he would have had to divorce the eldest of his wives, Mathila, to bring the number of his wives down to four again. This widow would have become the seventh in the line of his wives. The only thing that prevented him from fulfilling his desire was pity for my mother, who would have suffered a relapse if my father had embarked on fulfilling his idea. He abandoned his plan, considering this to be a sacrifice on his part for her sake, for she was the youngest of his wives and the one he loved most.

My father had eighteen sons and nine daughters. He once said to me, "The soul does not age, my son. The desire to seek what we have lost and yearn for remains hidden inside it, and when that desire flares up, it becomes a source of torment."

My father loved life, and now he was on the point of dying.

■

On the evening of the seventh day, the women of the clan came, dressed in black. They had heard the news before they assembled in the courtyard, as usual. My father breathed his last breaths before sunset, and word spread quickly through Ra's al-Naba' and the neighboring villages. The women of the clan remained kneeling around his corpse until morning, while the men of the clan asked for God's mercy for him and recalled his deeds in the guest room that now lacked its owner, leaving behind a considerable vacuum.

In the morning, we washed him, wrapped him in a sheet and covered him with a Palestinian flag. Six of his grandsons carried his bier on their shoulders, and we prepared for him a solemn funeral procession in which the clansmen walked with the people of Ra's al-Naba', with notables from Jerusalem and the surrounding villages, with my brother Falihan's in-laws, my sister Falha's husband and his relatives who lived in the al-'Awda camp. The women of the clan walked behind the formal procession, mourning him with sad voices, while the November rain came down gently from the sky.

> Open for Mannan the houses of might and nobility
> Mannan has come to you as a guest, people of the dead!

Tears flowed from my eyes as I recalled my promise to my father that I would unite the family and the clan. It was a thorny task that I could not fulfill, and had not expended any significant effort on, because at the bottom of my heart I was not convinced by it. My father wanted me to become a copy of himself. But this was not possible because the circumstances and times were so different.

One thing I did convey to him before he lost consciousness was that I had started to record the events in the life of the family and clan. Events that I had garnered from people older than myself, or that I had gleaned—and continue to draw—from stories and events related to me by my mother, as well as from experiences of my own life and the lives of the men and women of the family and the clan.

I looked into his eyes and a feeling of embarrassment came over me again. I saw the ghost of a smile on his face. I couldn't explain what it meant or concealed, but in a weak voice he said to me, "I am worn out, you go on!"

After a silence, he added, as if it was the only thing that concerned him at the end of his life, "*Bury me in a tomb next to the tomb of my mother.*"

Then he went into a long coma.

At that moment, I realized the enormity of the moment of parting, and felt that afterwards I'd be unable to cope.

My father Mannan died on Thursday evening, and we buried him on Friday morning.

About the Author

Mahmoud Shukair is a Palestinian writer, born in Jabal al-Mukabbar, Jerusalem, in 1941. The author of forty-five books, six television series, and four plays, his works include short stories and novels for adults and young adults, a volume of folktales, a biography of Jerusalem, and a travelogue. His stories have been translated into several languages, including English, French, German, Chinese, Korean, Mongolian, and Czech. For many years a teacher and journalist, he served as editor of the magazines *Al-Talia'a* [The Vanguard] and *Dafatir Thaqafiya* [Cultural File]. Mahmoud Shukair has occupied leadership positions within the Jordanian Writers' Union and the Union of Palestinian Writers and Journalists. He was jailed twice by Israeli authorities, for nearly two years, and in 2011 he was awarded the Mahmoud Darwish Prize for Freedom of Expression. He has spent his life between Beirut, Amman, Prague, and Jerusalem, where he now lives.